NINE MONTHS
AND NO MAN . . .

'But the child will have no father . . . '

'Millions of children have no father, and divil a bit of harm it does them. It's not the fact the child will have no father that matters in this fucking country, but the fact that I have no marriage certificate. What a nation of hypocrites we are! We all know that every year thousands of women getting married are pregnant, but as long as they have big white weddings and the priest blesses them, that's fine. It's not the sex outside marriage that is taboo in this country, it's being found out. If I had an abortion or had my baby adopted that would be fine. But by keeping it it is going to be a living proof that I broke the eleventh commandment: "Thou shalt not be found out".'

'Now you listen to me,' he cut in. 'Do you realise that keeping the baby practically rules out any chance of marriage?'

'Yes, I've thought about that,' I laughed wryly, 'Irishmen all want sex before marriage, but they want to marry virgins. It's a bit of a conundrum. Never mind, marriage has never been my top priority. And if I ever do think of marrying, it will be to a man who doesn't think that his prick is God's gift to women!'

. . . . THE SHOCKING STORY
OF AN IRISH PREGNANCY

Maura Richards was born in a small town in the South of Ireland in 1939. She worked at jobs in various parts of Ireland before coming to Dublin in 1968. Two years later her daughter was born, and in 1972 she helped to start Cherish, an association of single parents. In 1977 she married Graham Richards, a lecturer in psychology at the North-East London Polytechnic, and moved to live near Sevenoaks in Kent, in a five-hundred-year-old cottage. She completed the present book in 1979, while staying at the Oregon State University campus at Corvallis. She is currently working on a second book.

MAURA RICHARDS

TWO TO TANGO

WARD RIVER PRESS
DUBLIN

A Paperback Original
First published 1981 by
Ward River Press Ltd.,
Knocksedan House,
Swords, Co. Dublin, Ireland.

© Maura Richards 1981

ISBN 0 907085 09 1

Cover design by John Dixon
Printed by Cahill Printers Limited,
East Wall Road, Dublin 3.

I dedicate this book
TO ME

Contents

PART THREE

PART ONE

I

So I was going to die. And my baby would die too. It didn't seem to matter. I had never thought much about death, but when I did it was always with terror, trying to snatch my mind back from it. Promising myself that someday I would face it, someday I would sit down and have a real good think about death, but not yet. Now I didn't care, I was sliding into it gently, my mind clouding over, peace coming and rest, rest, I was so tired. The contractions were getting worse, but I had no energy now to get myself up and try to push, so we'd both die, maybe my baby was dead already.

Where was the nurse, why didn't somebody come? They wanted me to die, I knew, that's why they left me here alone. It was because I was an unmarried mother — they couldn't fool me. Now I understood, that's why there are no unmarried mothers in Ireland. Why hadn't I thought of it before? It was because they were all left to die when they were having their babies.

I must do something about it, then. They were killing all the unmarried mothers in Ireland. It was probably on the orders of the Catholic Church. There was a big conspiracy — I could see it all now. I'd have to get out of here and tell somebody . . .

'Oh fucking Jesus, why don't you stop the pain?' A scream tore from my lips as a huge contraction slammed into my lower back like a sledge hammer. Automatically

I tried to react and push, but it was no good. I fell back on the hard bed, hopeless, whimpering, wishing now that I could stay alive, but knowing it was too late, too late . . .

How long had I been here? Days? Weeks? Months? Years? Where was my child's father? Out fucking another woman?

'No, no, he's out buying a suit, he is buying a suit for seventy pounds, for seventy pounds, for seventy pounds, he's buying a suit for seventy pounds, and he won't give you a ha'penny . . . ' The chant went around in my head driving me mad.

Why was I here? God, why was I here, left to die, a mound of useless flesh on a hard bed in a nursing home in Dublin? Why did nobody care about me? Tears were trickling down my face, I knew, but I wasn't even crying. The tears were coming out on their own, full of sympathy for me, understanding how miserable I was. At least they understood, my tears did, nobody else in the whole world cared . . .

I remember when it all started, God I remember, it was a thousand years ago — no, nine hundred — the magic number nine. It was nine hundred years ago I got pregnant. For women who are approved of, pregnancy is only nine months, but for those of us outside the pale, it is nine hundred years.

I had woken up in my flat that morning nine hundred years ago and forced myself to face the fact that I might be pregnant. I had sat up in bed shaking with terror, trying again to pretend it hadn't happened, trying to push back the panic. I forced myself to take out a cigarette and light it, and watched like a mesmerized rabbit, my shaking hand trying to connect the match to the cigarette end. The panic was stupid, I assured myself. After all, my period was only one day overdue, but we had taken a chance a fortnight ago. Just once we had made love without taking precautions. But that was only once. I couldn't be pregnant after just once, but it had been at the wrong time, so I could be pregnant, we had made love right in the middle of the wrong time. Terrified I had jumped out of bed and reached for the calendar to count the days properly. The relief had been fantastic, I had been counting all wrong, my period wasn't due until the next week-end. I gave myself a good dressing down for being so stupid and set to doing the Saturday morning clean-up of my flat with energy.

I loved this house in which I lived, it was old and very gracious, set in a tree-lined road on the North side of the city. My bed-sit was beautiful. Big and airy, with a high ornate ceiling, a big window beside my bed which looked out over the garden. God, I loved it, if I had really been pregnant I'd probably have had to leave it. What an awful thought. I had gone about my work singing, refusing to admit that at the back of my mind there was a niggling worry.

The week had flown by at the office. Several times the ominous word 'pregnant' had crept out from the back of my mind, but I had pushed it firmly away, I was having no nonsense. That Friday two friends who worked with me, Susan and Joan, went down to Carlow for the week-end with me. The last thing I did before leaving the flat was stick a packet of STs in my bag, I knew I'd need them before the night was out. We loved getting out of Dublin for the week-end.

Helen and I had shared a flat in Carlow a few years ago and she still lived there — it was like going home. There was always a party of one kind or another. Not that the parties were organized; usually people just dropped in, brought a jar. Sing-songs would start without a bit of bother. The talent was usually great, not that there were fantastic singing voices, though some were good, it was more in the way a story would be told, a yarn spun out.

One of the lads, who couldn't hold two notes together to save his life, always insisted on singing the 'Gipsy Rover' — all twenty-two verses of it. If he missed a line at the tenth verse he always went back and started over again. No matter how often he did it he always had us rolling round the floor laughing.

That week-end it seemed as if people had turned up

from all over the country. The crack was great. The dawn was poking her fingers through the slits of the venetian blinds when we finally dragged ourselves to bed on Sunday morning, having talked through the night and settled the problems of the world at large.

It was always easier to solve the problems of the world at large, I mused, as we drove to Dublin on Monday morning. It was different when they became particular — like what for instance was I going to do about my period which still had not come.

II

I got through three more days. On Thursday night Jennifer came down to ask me to drive her to have her cards read by Gipsy Lee. I was glad to do it, anything to keep my mind occupied. I was standing on the fender, craning to see myself in the mirror over the fireplace and Jennifer was wandering around the room, aimlessly flicking through magazines, when she suddenly wheeled around and said,

'By the way, I meant to tell you, I had to go to the doctor to-day, I haven't had a period for two months and he said I was completely run down.'

I stood, one foot on the fender, the lipstick suspended half way to my mouth, watching myself in the mirror. The lines of anxiety just fell off my face. So that's what it was all about. I knew Jennifer wasn't pregnant and of course it was quite on the cards that not only was I run down, but that I hadn't a drop of blood in my body anyway. I could have hugged Jennifer. I practically danced out to the car as we set off to consult the famous Gipsy.

Gipsy Lee lived just off Dorset Street and several of my women friends got me to drive them down to see her about once a month. I always sat in the car while they went in. Wild horses wouldn't get me to have my fortune told. I had a holy horror of fortune tellers. But that night was different, that night I could have faced fifty fortune tellers sitting in a row. Jennifer was a bit puzzled at how easily I agreed to go up with her, not knowing that after the weight she had lifted off my mind, I'd have made a good try at going up a steeple with her there and then had she asked me.

The Gipsy's flat was on the second floor of a huge complex owned by the Corporation. We climbed the stone steps and down a long balcony, with all the closed doors on our left, an icy wind whipping into our faces from the courtyard around which the complex was built. There were timid lights shining outside each door and we finally found the number we wanted.

Jennifer knocked and the door was opened by a boy of about six, who without saying a word to us, brought us down the tiny hallway and showed us into a sitting-room where he left us, closed the door and disappeared.

All I can remember about that room is that it was crazily cluttered with furniture and potted plants and pictures. There was just a small space clear in the middle of the room, and a few straight-backed dining-chairs and a sofa made a semi-circle on the edge of the clutter. We made room for ourselves on the sofa, most of which was piled high with clothes. Opposite us on one of the straight chairs was another client, a woman, obviously completely at home. She was definitely what one would call a solid citizen. Not so much fat as substantial, and with the well satisfied look of a woman who knows her place in the world. This woman was not into surprises, I reckoned. Surprises wouldn't be her cup of tea at all. She had on a good brown fur coat, with a silk scarf barely protruding at the neck, a brown pill-box type felt hat, sat firmly on well kept grey hair. Black leather medium heeled court shoes, black leather gloves and the enormous square black leather handbag held firmly on her lap all portrayed a woman of substance.

She stared at us without blinking. The space between us was too small for any private conversation, so we just stared back. Without warning she spoke.

'If yez came to see the Gipsy,' she said, 'yez are wastin' yer time, she's not on tonight, didn't Jamsie tell yez?' We didn't get time even to shake our heads.

'Ah, well, never mind, Imelda is on, yez are lucky 'tis Imelda, she's much better than th'other wan. Personally of course I always goes to the Gipsy — ah yez can't bate the Gipsy — she's given me nothing but the best advice these past ten year, built me business up on the Gipsy's advice so I did, never buys a bit of stocks nor shares unless I asks her first.'

I was looking at her in astonishment. The idea of this woman buying stocks and shares and building up a good business on the advice of a fortune teller fascinated me. I liked the fact that she didn't try to upgrade her accent in accordance with her financial improvement. She was sound Dublin working class, certainly with middle class leanings, but not ashamed of her background; in other clothes she could easily be one of Behan's shawlies. It also seemed more probable to me that she came here from Nolan's pub rather than from the devotions in the church across the road. I was wrong.

'Just come from the novena,' she said as if she had read my mind. 'Ah, a grand man, Father Daly, but won't be long here d'ye know, sez out too much, makes too much critizals of the powers that be — aye, himself is a hard task master when it comes to the young priests, a hard task master.'

She lapsed into a sad silence. I was dying to ask who 'himself' was, was it God, or the Archbishop of Dublin she was talking about. Certainly the Archbishop had a reputation for treating his priests badly. Before I could ask she was continuing her monologue.

'Aye, I comes here about once a week, after the novena. It's all right to be praying ye know, but it's good to have the bit of inside information — them stocks is very confusin', very confusin' . . . '

She sighed, burdened with the weight of all the business she had to transact. The fact that the church had things to say about fortune tellers bothered her not at all. She was becoming more and more contradictory, and I was dying to ask her some questions, but the boy opened the door, held it for her and she went out without another word. Jennifer and I looked at each other in bewilderment.

'Let's get the hell out of here', I said, deciding the place was even more daft than I had thought, 'you can't seriously pay money to listen to this rubbish.'

'Please,' Jennifer said, 'let's stay, it's only a bit of fun, you can come in with me, I'll even pay the ten bob for a palm reading for you — how about that?'

III

Imelda was even younger than I expected. She was lovely looking, with long straight dark hair and an air of innocence about her which made the whole situation even more ridiculous — two grown women paying a child to tell them their fortunes. She bent over my palm and stared at it intently as if she could really read something in it. Then she started speaking slowly, as if she was in some kind of trance.

'You have a sunny nature which helps you to overcome a lot of life's problems,' she intoned in a solemn voice.

'Christ', I thought, 'I'll do for Jennifer when I get her out of here. Imagine listening to this kind of tripe.' Still I couldn't help chuckling at the idea that I must tell our sales manager about my 'sunny nature' because usually his first greeting when I entered his office was, 'For God's sake girl, will you go away and haunt someone else.' I was smiling to myself, thinking about what he'd say about my 'sunny nature' and hardly listening to Imelda at all. Then the marrow in my bones froze.

'Somebody in your family has just become pregnant and is trying to keep it a secret.' Had I heard the words? Did she really say them? The ice was beginning to spill out of the marrow and spread all over my body. I was turning to stone. I wondered would they somehow be able to discover that I had been pregnant when I turned to stone. Maybe someone with a chisel would find out. And then I started to melt, oh God, I was going to melt away completely and be just a drop of water running away on the floor. I was conscious that all the time I was standing there with my hand held out, a faint look of interest in my face, then I was sitting down and she was telling Jennifer about dark men and long journeys over water. At last we were in the car and I reached for the inevitable cigarette. And then it came.

'Who was she talking about expecting in your family, and even if they were, why on earth would they want to keep it a secret?' A very good question, why on earth would they want to keep it a secret?

Somehow I parried the questions on the way home. Jennifer was obsessed with the person in my family who could possibly be keeping a pregnancy a secret. She knew all my family and was going through a long question and answer session with herself, ruling my sisters and sisters-in-law out one by one. I tried to put her off, telling her she was daft to pay attention to a sixteen year old girl and that she should have more sense for herself. By the time we got to her door my nerves were completely stretched and I badly needed to be alone. I refused to go in for coffee, pleading a bad headache and finally said goodnight to Jennifer. But then I couldn't go home — what had that fortune teller meant? Had she really read something in my palm?

I drove around aimlessly, until I realised I was near the home of a friend who lived in Cabra. Betty was a widow with four fairly grown up children and at least I could talk to her. When I went in she was on her own, sitting watching telly. I just stood there in the middle of the floor staring, until eventually she said,

'For heaven's sake, Bríg O'Mahony, will you sit down or go home, but stop standing there like an image.'

'I'm pregnant!' Somebody said those words somewhere in the room, of course it wasn't me, but somebody did say them. I don't know what reaction I expected, but it surely wasn't what I got. Betty was in knots laughing.

'What are you talking about, you bloody eejit?' she

said.

'I'm pregnant. Gipsy Lee's niece Imelda has just told me that I'm pregnant.' If I had been less serious the expression on her face would have been comical. Sheer disbelief was registered followed by a half idea that in fact I was serious.

'Look, for God's sake sit down and tell me what you are talking about.'

I told her, ending with what the fortune teller had said.

'But are you pregnant? Did you take a chance? And where is Eric?'

Good God, I'd forgotten all about Eric. It must be the shock that had blanked him out of my mind. He had been away for two weeks and wouldn't be back for another two. Was I going daft? How had I not thought about him up to now? It was as if somehow he had nothing to do with the situation.

Betty was talking, what was she saying? I tried to concentrate on what she was saying. . . .

'There's a doctor that I know, ring him up now and make an appointment to see him tomorrow. He'll give you pills to make your period come, or else he'll tell you how to get an abortion in England, and if you are going to have an abortion, now is the time to have it. Did you have a hot bath?'

Now I was looking at her as if she had two heads.

'I have a bath nearly every night, what in hell's name has that to do with anything?'

'Look, dopey,' she said with exaggerated patience, 'on your way home go into a pub, right?, buy a bottle of gin, go home and fill the bath with water as hot as you can possibly bear it, take off your clothes and sit in the bath and drink the bottle of gin, now do you think you can manage that? My God what kind of a fucking fool are you? Will you do what I tell you and if your period hasn't come tomorrow, see that doctor and ring me tomorrow night . . . '

The gin was standing on the end of the bath, I had wandered into a bar and bought it on the way home from

Betty's. It was good C.D.C. gin. I stood beside the bath which was full of boiling water and tried to make up my mind. Did I swallow the gin first, or get into the bath first? Now I could barely see the bottle through the haze of steam. I was nearly fainting already from lack of air. I must get into the bath, it was like an inferno. I put one foot in and had to pull it out again, I couldn't bear the pain. I stepped straight back in and sat down. A scream started at the back of my throat and I had to put my wrist into my mouth and bite hard to stop the noise. I sat there for about two seconds glaring at the bottle of gin through a mist of pain and vapour and then I couldn't bear it any longer. I must get out, I practically threw myself over the side of the bath and staggered into my room. From my neck to my toes was one lump of raw flesh. I felt as if every piece of skin had been stripped off my body.

IV

I woke next morning with a feeling of terrible catastrophe. For a split second my mind was blank and then memory came rushing back — the bath, the gin. Oh God, if Edith saw it she'd surely guess. I rushed out to the bathroom. The water was still in the bath, grey and cold and sinister looking, as if it held some dark secret of mine which it could tell at any time. I pulled the plug out and let the viscous thing rush away. The gin bottle still stood mockingly. I unscrewed the cork and emptied the gin into the quickly disappearing water.

What had I tried to do last night? Had I tried to kill something? Well, at least I hadn't succeeded. Was there a feeling of relief somewhere that in fact the hot bath hadn't worked? Was I glad then that I was pregnant? Was I gone completely out of my already mad mind?

'I am not going to talk about it now,' I practically screamed out loud at the other part of myself which wouldn't shut up. 'I'll talk about it tonight, tonight I'll work it all out, to-day I am not pregnant, I'm not going to be pregnant, I don't want to be pregnant, now shut up.'

I was still standing beside the empty bath with the empty gin bottle in my hand. I stuck it into the basket, where in my odd fits of tidiness I put clothes to be washed and promptly forgot all about them. The last place I would ever think of looking for clothes for washing was in a laundry basket, just as the last place to look for tea was in a canister marked 'tea'. I always took it for granted that a word marked on the outside of a tin or jar or file was a clue to something, rather than a description of the contents, which could account for the fact that I spent half of my life looking for things that were right under my nose.

I must get to work. All my working life I had got up at 9.30 or ten o'clock to be at work at nine. Over the years I had tried all kinds of tricks to encourage me to get out of bed. Fast clocks, slow clocks, clocks in tin cans at the other end of the room, people calling me, everything had failed and finally I had come to the conclusion that I must live with this affliction. I eased my conscience by working late, or Saturdays or Sundays as the need arose, and except for periodic explosions with my employer, it worked out fairly well.

It was now a quarter to ten, I'd be in by ten o'clock, not too bad. I had brought the business of getting from my bed to the office to a fine art and in ten minutes I was sitting behind my desk. There hadn't been anyone looking for me so there were no problems. I stuck to my work with a concentration that excluded any stray thoughts, and I succeeded pretty well, until half way through the afternoon, and then the inevitability of what I had to face once work was over started to loom again. I was saved by the phone. A friend of Joan's was over from Glasgow for a few days, and asked me out for a meal that evening. I accepted gladly — anything to put off the evil hour.

Ben picked me up at 7.30 at the flat and we decided on the Waldorf on the quays for a meal. The food was good and the wine was good, and I chattered as brightly as a sparrow for two hours and then suddenly the effort began to fail and I decided I wasn't feeling well and wanted an early night anyway. I asked Ben in for a cup of coffee and as we sat one on each side of the fire drinking it, it was becoming increasingly difficult for me to even pretend to follow the conversation and then I realised that there had been silence for several seconds and that Ben's eyes were riveted on my face on which all my misery was nakedly exposed. I tried to pull back the mask, but it was no use.

'What on earth is wrong with you?' Ben asked gently, 'I've been watching you all evening and there's something bothering you, tell me.'

I stared at him, I knew he was waiting for an answer. What would he say if I told him? Would the look of concern leave his face? Would he despise me? And then a strangled voice that I knew must be mine said the words.

'I'm pregnant.' They hung in the air between us. I could see them and I knew they were a reality. Ben came and sat on the arm of my chair and held me, and then I started crying, except that I wasn't crying, I was whimpering like a hurt animal.

'Are you sure you are pregnant?' he said, 'have you been to the doctor?'

'No, I haven't been to the doctor, but I know.'

'But what are you going to do?'

'I don't know, I don't know, oh God, I don't know.'

'Have you told Eric?'

Eric. Eric. Why did I keep forgetting him? I remembered now, Ben had met him.

'No I haven't told him, he's away until the weekend.'

'But surely you can get married, I mean what's all the big problem?'

'Eric and I have never talked about getting married and I honestly don't think I could make pregnancy a basis for marriage.'

'But surely you're not thinking of having the baby yourself and not being married. Do you realise what you are talking about? The child would be illegitimate, a bastard! You can't do that to a child, you've got to have an abortion!'

Abortion, there it was again, it seemed to be the only answer. Ben was talking again.

'Can you have one here in Ireland? Would your doctor do it for you?'

The sound of my laughter was slightly hysterical. Instinctively, the one thing I knew my doctor would never encourage me to do was to have an abortion.

'Well then, go to England,' Ben said, 'It's not difficult,

it will be all over in a week. You've got the rest of your life to think about. What would you do with a child?'

I told him about the doctor Betty knew.

'Well promise me you'll go and see him tomorrow and make all the arrangements. The quicker it's done the better.'

I promised, tomorrow I'd make all the arrangements to get rid of whatever it was that was inside me.

'Please Ben, go away from me now.' Suddenly I wanted to be alone. I could feel his kindness and concern for me; he hadn't rejected me or turned away and somehow it gave me heart. Reluctantly he went, and at the door again he made me promise to see the doctor about the arrangements. The next day I promised myself I'd go the day after. That evening when I got in from work there was a letter for me from the Intercontinental Hotel.

By now you have probably made up your mind what you intend to do about your problems. You are a very strong-willed girl and I'm sure that whatever choice you make will be the correct one for you. In case you may be considering a short trip to the U.K. for therapeutic reasons (and I'm not being facetious) the enclosed article may be of interest to you.

Yours sincerely
Ben

The 'sincerely' was underlined. The article was from an English paper and was on a new method of aborting women under three months pregnant. It was all so easy. All I had to do was go to England. How long would it take? Three or four days, a week at the most, and then it would be all over and this nightmare would be finished with.

I would have to get some money someplace, at least a few hundred pounds. Where on earth would I borrow that much money? I didn't have two pennies to rub together, and as it was I owed the bank about three hundred pounds. There was very little possibility of getting more money out of them. Where would I go then? To Eric of course, he had plenty of money.

Why did I keep pushing Eric out of my mind, as if it all had nothing whatever to do with him? Why was there such a blank? Such a nothingness, and where was all the warmth, and the love and the caring gone? And there was caring, I cared very much about Eric and he about me. OK, so we had never talked about marriage, but what about that, we had only been together for a few months. I must go to Eric, of course I must go to him.

He was back in town since yesterday. I knew because Edith had told me he had been looking for me and I had caught the surprised look on her face when I hadn't reacted as usual.

V

I met him coming out his own door. He wrapped his arms around me in his usual bear hug, and for a second everything between us was as it had always been, except that it wasn't and I just didn't know why. With our arms around each other we walked back to his flat. Normally it would be an occasion for frantic love making, but now I was restless, I broke away and wandered around the flat with Eric following, running his fingertips lightly over my body in a way that would usually drive me sexually wild. But I couldn't react. I felt cold and dead inside me. I turned around and looked at Eric. He stood across the room, big and bronzed and beautiful, as they say in the women's magazines. Vitality seemed to ooze from him. I had worried myself sick for the past three weeks and there he stood with not a care in the world. It was obvious that his greatest problem at the moment was my sudden reluctance — and how the hell he was going to get me into bed.

I stared at him as if he were a complete stranger. I felt as though I could never bear to make love to him again. There was an atmosphere building up between us and I knew it was my fault, somehow or other I was creating it, I didn't know how or why, but I knew I was doing it and I must stop it. I must tell Eric the whole thing this minute and stop the stupid rubbish that was going on in my head. I turned to tell him, but instead started talking about his trip. Sexually, at least, that turned him off for a while — he always got vocal about his work. As usual I kidded him about the blondes he must have met while he was away. Why was it always blondes men were supposed to meet while they were away, I wondered? Vaguely I began to think that as far as their image was concerned, blondes got a very raw deal.

'You know you're the only blonde for me,' Eric was saying in a voice that would melt a frozen mummy.

Of course I knew, I never had any other men, so why should he have other women? For me it was as simple as that. I was hungry, I decided, so Eric started throwing a meal together as only he could. He always did the cooking. Once he had told me that I couldn't cook, he had never had to tell me twice. I had never liked cooking, though I was not the extreme kind who tried to open an egg with a tin opener. Now Eric was singing away as he hurled all kinds of things into a pot. On our cosy evenings as we called them, when we just stayed home and ignored all visitors we would shed our clothes and then hop into the bath together. This always ended up with me pretending to scream blue murder, because while Eric was quite willing to cook, cleaning was my province and the bathroom was always in a shocking mess since we usually ended up making dripping wet love all over the place. Then Eric would produce one of his concoctions out of all the pots and pans, we'd pull our huge bed into a strategic place in front of the television, which we did in fact happen to see sometimes, but usually on these occasions we made love and talked and smoked and dozed and made love again until we were exhausted. It was always so marvellous.

Eric broke into my reverie by kissing me on the nose.

'You look so happy, darling, earlier I thought there was something wrong with you.'

I came back to reality with a jerk.

'Eric, I've got to talk to you,' I blurted. He had laid out our meal on the table and sat down. For once I could have done without the candles and the blaring music, was he stone deaf, or tone deaf?

'Eric, for God's sake turn down that music,' I begged, 'I've got to speak to you.'

I stared at him in silence, I knew my eyes were pleading with him to know what I wanted to say, but he just sat at the other side of the table, matter of factly waiting for me to speak so that he could get on with his meal. How had I gotten myself into this situation? How could I, at thirty years of age, be sitting like a tongue-tied teenager incapable of telling this stranger opposite me that I was carrying his baby. STRANGER. The word stood out in capital letters. That was the answer. He was a stranger. If I were honest, I had to admit I knew very little about him. I had met him at a party one night and hadn't particularly noticed him until he asked me to dance. That was it; I loved to dance — he was a perfect dancer. The rest has been told a million times in every popular romance, we danced and dined and drank and fucked our way through six months of — what? Nothing.

'Fucking nothing!' I shouted out loud and glared at the look of enquiry on his face. 'Oh, it doesn't matter,' I practically barked as I shot up from the table, not having eaten anything.

'Oh, it doesn't matter,' I practically barked as I shot up from the table.

'I thought you were hungry, Brig,' Eric said, following me.

'Yes, I was hungry, now I'm not hungry, is that OK? Or do I have to be hungry just because you cooked a meal?'

'Darling, you don't have to be anything', there was real concern in his voice now. 'Sit down, there is something wrong with you, I'll get you a drink.'

'I'll have a glass of water.'

'Water! When there's good brandy in the house? My God, you are sick.'

Dear Jesus, I was going to go stark staring mad in two seconds, he was pretending. He couldn't be that thick. A blind fool would know what was wrong with me.

'There's nothing wrong with me, Eric, absolutely nothing,' I said in my most controlled voice, 'I'm just a bit off colour, I'll be all right.'

'OK, I'll tell you what, we'll go up to the local and have a quiet jar, eh?'

'All right, Eric, we'll go up to the local and have a quiet jar.'

The 'quiet jar' was a disaster. Any casual observer must surely have been able to read the scene at a glance. I felt I must look like a fish resting against a stream, with my mouth half opening and closing periodically, except that a fish in a stream was a restful thing, I thought grimly. My mind was in turmoil. How in God's name had this situation developed between Eric and myself I thought, why hadn't I told him the minute I met him to-day that I thought I was pregnant? Why was I building this bloody atmosphere between us? I'd tell him now, be quite casual about it. The fish's mouth half opened again and closed. No sound came out.

Suddenly I was running out of the pub with Eric hard on my heels. Outside the door he swung me around on my heels and shook me.

'Are you gone mad? Do you realise that our drinks are still in there?'

'I don't care, I don't care, do you hear? I want to go home.'

The silence shouted at us all the way up the road and into the flat. Scarcely had he closed the door when I turned to him.

'Eric, I'm pregnant.' The words came out in a breathless rush and then the tension began to ease out of my body. I leaned against the wall and every nerve began to unwind. Everything would be all right now. Eric knew, he'd fix everything, he'd come and put his arms around me now and hold me and mind me and take away all the fear. Oh God, just to rest in his arms and know that everything would be all right. I should have told him before, silly ass . . . Suddenly my eyes flew open. Where was Eric, why hadn't he come to me? He was standing pouring drinks as casually as if I'd told him it was raining outside.

'So you think you are pregnant, huh? How long are

you overdue?'

How long was I overdue? Something niggled at the back of my mind about the way he asked that question, but I couldn't think what it was.

'About three weeks, my period is about three weeks late.'

'Ah, you're making a big fuss about nothing, you couldn't know in three weeks.'

He was turning away, putting on the radio, something was wrong, where was the loving and cuddling and caring I had been waiting for? Eric didn't understand, I must tell him again properly, he thought I was joking, I must keep my voice calm.

'Eric, darling, do you realise what I said, I think I'm pregnant, I think I'm going to have a baby, your baby.' Why was there such silence? Why didn't he say something?

'Eric, what am I going to do?'

'Do? What do you mean, what are you going to do? What does every woman do? Go and have an abortion.'

This wasn't real, this was a nightmare, I wasn't really here telling Eric I was going to have his baby, he wasn't really standing across the room casually telling me to have an abortion, it was all a bad dream. I must wake up, what did one do to break a bad nightmare? Move one's tongue around in one's mouth? That usually did it, but no matter what I did I was still standing where I was and Eric was still standing across the room from me. I must approach this thing differently, make Eric realise that I had been through three weeks of hell, I must be calm and matter-of-fact.

'Eric, suppose I am pregnant, I haven't the money to have an abortion. I'd have to go to England and it would cost about a hundred and fifty pounds.'

'But I'll give you the money, of course I'll give you the money, of course I'll give you the money, you little ass.' Suddenly he was holding me gently and I leaned against him with relief. I was an awful amadán, for a while there I thought Eric didn't care, of course he cared, he cared just as much as I did. For the first time in three weeks I was nearly happy. I relaxed against him and my body began to come alive under the gentle caressing of his hands.

Hours later, as I lay awake smoking a cigarette, it suddenly dawned on me that we had made love about three times without taking any precautions. So I really was pregnant, and what's more Eric knew it just as well as I did. For the first time in our relationship I slipped out of bed and got dressed without waking him. He was sleeping soundly and didn't move as I went quietly out of the flat.

VI

Edith was knocking at the door. Oh God, did I have to wake up? Why couldn't I just die or something and not have to cope with this problem which refused to go away?

'It's ten o'clock, are you getting up for work?' Edith called from outside the door.

'Come in, Edith. No, I won't go to work to-day, I feel a bit under the weather.'

In her early days Edith's family had had lots of money and servants all over the place. She had never had to work to earn her living and insisted that 'all you young things' as she called anyone under fifty, 'work far too hard in those horrible offices, and then trying to keep a hectic social life going as well.'

This was why when one wanted a day in bed one never had to pretend to Edith that one was sick. As far as she was concerned all us young people who bravely held down these terrible nine-to-five jobs were entitled to all the days in bed we could get. Darling Edith, since I had come to the house two years ago, she had been like a mother to me. She was the youngest seventy-six-year-old I had ever met, and was one of the few people of her generation who constantly sang the praises of the young people of to-day. One of the few things that irritated her was our apparent claim to have discovered sex, contraception and all the rest.

'Good heavens' she would say, 'I don't understand why you young people think you invented sex. We knew all about it in my day, you know, we whispered to each other about how we planned our families, but we didn't think it necessary to blaze it across the front page of the *Times*.'

The only difference Edith could see between her generation and ours was the fact that we put everything on the front page of the *Times*. Another thing that bothered her greatly was people's ages.

'In my young day, one didn't ask another person his or her age. Now if the woman down the road falls off her bike and hurts her ankle, you read in the paper next day, Miss So-and-So (56) fell off her bike and hurt her ankle. Now I ask you, what has the poor woman's age to do with falling off her bike — and she might have been keeping it a secret for years, and there it is all over the *Times*.'

She came in now, bringing me a cup of tea, and then went off to ring the office and tell them in a voice that brooked no contradiction that I was absolutely incapable of coming to the office to-day. If she had only known it she was quite right; I felt totally incapable of doing anything. I knew I was safe for the rest of the day. Edith would assume I was sleeping and would not come near me and wouldn't let anyone else disturb me either, so I had the whole day to sort out my problem somehow.

And then suddenly I didn't seem to have a problem. All I had to do was to go and see this particular doctor this evening. He would arrange to have me in a clinic in London by the week-end and I'd be back probably early next week. Eric would give me the money and probably come with me as well, so the whole thing was solved. Why then did I feel like some kind of a dead thing? I tried to sleep and dozed fitfully for several hours.

Then I was sitting up in bed wide awake, and I knew, I knew I wasn't going to have an abortion, and I knew why. It was the girl, the girl in the office, no she wasn't in the office, it was about a year ago, suddenly the fellows were getting into huddles and there were lots of comings and goings and peculiar phone calls. I had a little office of my own well tucked away, and lots of things went on that I never heard about at all. However eventually I had dis-covered that a girl whom some of the men knew was pregnant, and I gathered they were all in a panic in case one of them should be named as the father. One day I got hold of one of them and tackled him. He was a decent type and I couldn't quite understand his attitude. He told me that the girl was living at home and would be murdered by her parents if they ever found out, so she had to leave home but at the moment she didn't have any place to go. I remembered that I was just going to tell him to ask her to come and live with me, and then feeling embarrassed at thinking she might have nobody else to help her, I shut my mouth. That was the end of the episode until several months later I suddenly asked Richard how his friend was getting on.

'Oh, she went to England and got rid of it,' he said casually. 'Cost her a packet, she's been pretty cut up about it since too.'

Sitting up in bed now, I distinctly remembered the sick feeling of guilt that hit me, guilt because I could have held out a hand and didn't, and the feeling of useless destruction, of what, I wasn't quite sure. I could clearly remember Richard's astonished face as I told him viciously to get to hell out of the office, as if he somehow had added to my sense of guilt. Now the hopelessness which I had banished a few hours ago was back again. It was best that I go to England, why had I remembered that girl? I could be rid of the whole thing in . . .

'Rid of what?' the other half of me pounced as if it had been lurking somewhere waiting for me to make just that statement.

'What exactly are you getting rid of?'

'The makings of a baby.'

'Oh, the makings of a baby, just, and when in your considered opinion might the makings actually turn into a baby, then?'

'I don't know, at about three months, maybe. It's safe

to have an abortion up to three months.'

'Ah! so what's nothing suddenly becomes a baby at three months, that's really scientific. I'll tell you why you were so upset about that girl having an abortion. It's because you felt that a life was being snuffed out, that a child was being killed. You know damn well that you don't really believe that what's inside in you now is just nothing, but you're too much of a coward to admit it. Just tell me something, what right have you to decide that someone won't live, won't breathe and laugh and love and sing, yes and suffer too, because that's what it's all about, isn't it? You've seen a fair bit of misery in your life, but have you ever been sorry you were born? Have you ever in your life met anyone who has actually said they regretted been born? No, and will I tell you why, because it's all there is, it's the only challenge. For Christ's sake girl, take yourself aside and have a little chat with yourself and stop sitting there like a snivelling snail bent on destruction because you haven't the wit to think of anything more positive.'

At last the argument inside my head stopped. I was sitting crouched on the bed with my hands held in front of my face as if warding off blows. Never since I was very young had I ever been allowed to fool myself for any length of time. My other half, as I thought of it, had always stood cynically by and stripped me of any pretence. I had really been hoping to go and have an abortion before I had time to think, but it was too late now, that game was up, I now had to sit still and face the situation on the basis that what was inside me was life.

So now what? The black panic was hitting me again, coming up in wave after wave of fear. I must stop the panic. I lay down flat on the floor and spread out my arms and legs and forced my mind to go blank. Slowly the shaking stopped and my muscles began to relax. I stayed that way, lying on my belly with my face against the hard floor until I was completely calm. Now I must think, I had the whole afternoon to stay in that room and decide what I was going to do. If I wasn't going to have an abortion,

I needn't go to England until about April or May, I could work until the baby was due and then come home afterwards . . .

'What do you mean afterwards? After what? Do you realise you are going to have a baby? A child? What are you going to do, leave it on somebody's doorstep in England and come back here to get on with your own life?'

I hadn't thought about what I was going to do when the baby was born. I had just thought about getting through nine months, but after nine months there would be another person, a helpless baby, demanding love and care and protection. What did other women do? There must be other women, did they all go to England and what did they do there, where did all the babies go? No, they didn't all go to England, only a few weeks ago it had been in the *Times*, 'so many illegitimate children born last year,' then where were they, why did no one ever hear of them? Illegitimate! Oh God, if Eric didn't marry me my child would be illegitimate. Oh God, God, God, help me, why doesn't somebody help me? Had I been screaming out loud, had Edith heard me? I listened, there wasn't a sound in the house, the noise must only have been in my head.

'Look, why do you have to go to England?' The brains trust was back again.

'Because where else can I go, what else can I do, who ever heard of anyone being pregnant and single in Ireland?'

'What about the woman up the road that Edith is always talking about, who had a baby thirty years ago and whose parents put her out in the snow, but she held on to the child and reared him and now he's a fine young man who's doing very well for himself. Look, will I tell you why you want to run away to England? Because you're afraid, afraid of talk, afraid of what your friends will say, afraid of the neighbours, and for what? In the name of the good Christ, will you stand up on your feet girl and pull yourself together. Do you know that you are thinking of going through the misery of living in England on your own, and of giving away your child, or rearing it in England because

40

of talk? You've always lived in this country because you've wanted to, you've always paid tax since you started working, you've never taken tuppence from the State and now for the first time when you really need this country, you're going to run away. You need this place, you need your friends, you won't survive in England. Look, try to be honest, if any other one of the women came to you and told you she was pregnant what would you say?'

Without any hesitation the answer came.

'Stay put, have your baby and keep it and to hell with the begrudgers.'

'Right, like a good girl, take a bit of your own advice.'

VII

I knew immediately what I would do. I would go down to my own doctor straight away and find out. I had to know, had to be sure. He only lived a few doors away and I knew he'd be there by six o'clock. The shaking started again, I couldn't face him, what would he say? Stop thinking and move. He'd say I was a whore. Would he throw me out? Stop thinking, run the bath, hurry. Did he ever have another girl who was single and pregnant? What would I say? 'Doctor, I have a problem.' No — say it straight out — stop thinking. 'Doctor, I think I'm pregnant.' Oh no! Oh God I couldn't say that.

No, I wouldn't go to-day, I'd go tomorrow, there was no need to panic, tomorrow would do.

'You will go now, you bitch, stop thinking, just move.' I was nearly ready, what did I have to do next? — a sample, oh hell one couldn't have a pregnancy test without a sample! I found a baby Power bottle and stood staring at it, how in the name of God was one supposed to piddle into a baby Power bottle? It couldn't be done. Forget the whole thing.

'Look, thick, if you can't figure out how to get a sample into that bottle you're not even fit to be pregnant. Of course it can be done, other women must do it, so you do it.' I did it . . .

The yarn kept running through my mind about the two old women from the Coombe who ended up in court having beaten each other around the street.

'Madam, will you explain to me how this sorry state of affairs came about?' asked the Judge in his most precise voice.

'Well 'twas like this, yer honour,' said one. 'I was going along the street to see me doctor with me sample in me hand when I met Maggie.'

' "What's in the bottle, dear?" sez she.'

' "Urine," sez I.'

' "What?" sez she.'

' "Urine", sez I.'

' "What?" sez she.'

' "Piss", sez I.'

' "Well shit!" sez she, and that's how it all started.'

I wrapped the bottle in brown paper and put it down into the bottom of my bag. Now go, quickly, out the door and down the steps, one foot and then the other – my feet were made of lead, they wouldn't move. Make them move – one step, two steps, one step, two steps – what would he say? – don't think, just move – turn in the gate, up the steps, ring the bell.

The clang of the bell seemed to wake me from a trance. The door opened and he was standing there himself.

'Ah so it's yourself, is it? It's so long since I've seen you I thought you were left the country!'

'I think I might have to.'

'Oh so that's the way it is, is it? Go straight into the surgery.'

I sat on the edge of a chair as if every bone in my body had gone brittle and the slightest move on my part would shatter every one of them. My eyes were fixed firmly on the floor, I hardly breathed as I waited for the onslaught.

'So you're pregnant, are you?'

'Yes . . . '

'I see.' There was a long pause. He moved over to the window staring out, with his back to me. After forever, he turned back and stood beside me.

'Well you're not going to England, you are not having an abortion, you are staying here and keeping your child and

43

we'll look after you.'

My eyes flew to his face, how did he know exactly what I had been contemplating? There was nothing on his face but kindness and a look that said there would be no nonsense.

'Lift up your jumper till I feel your breasts, hmmm.' He barely touched them. 'Yes, they are fine and firm.'

I had known that myself, my breasts were always hopeless and then suddenly they had become quite rounded and hard.

'Are you going to examine me?'

'No, there's no need, I know you are pregnant and you know, but you can take that sample out of your bag and leave it with me.'

My God, the man was a magician. 'How did you know what was in my bag?'

'Of course I know, and I bet you it is in a small whiskey bottle wrapped in brown paper.'

Silently I handed him the bottle. 'Have you had other women in this situation, then?'

'Of course! Do you seriously think you are the only woman in Ireland who has ever been pregnant and not married? Have a bit of sense, girl, you're not that unusual.'

'Do any of them keep their babies?'

'Some do, some don't, are you going to marry the father?'

'No, he never asked me, he thinks I'm going to have an abortion.'

'The bastard!' The word was like a whiplash, all of a sudden the kindness was gone and he was pacing around like a caged cat. 'These young bucks, they should be horsewhipped, horsewhipped. Before you know where you are, he'll be boasting to his friends that he has you up the pole, or else he will deny the fact altogether.'

'No, no, you don't understand, he's not like that, he's a decent man, he'd never deny his own child. You shouldn't say such a thing, of course he'll support me, he has already offered me the money for the abortion!'

'Oh, he will do that all right, let's hope he continues

44

to do it when he knows you are going to keep the baby.'

'Of course he will, I wish you wouldn't talk like that, you don't know Eric, anyway isn't there some way of proving it, blood or something?'

'I wish there was, child, so that we could shorten the jockstraps of a lot of these lads and make them face some responsibility. Look, come back on Wednesday night at seven o'clock and I will tell you definitely, but I think we are both pretty sure, aren't we?'

'Yes, I think so.'

'Will there be somebody down in that flat?'

'Yes, yes, I'll be all right.'

'Ring me if you want anything or if you want to talk, but don't worry, we'll take care of you.'

'Thank you.' I knew he was standing at the door as I dragged my legs down the steps. It was as if he was trying to force strength into me. Consciously I lifted my head. Anyway after all, I was still not absolutely sure and anything could happen in two days.

The next morning I woke with the usual black blanket of disaster forcing itself down on top of me. Every morning was the same now, an instant of peace on waking, then the blackness and despair of realising the situation. On the way to work it dawned on me that I had a nagging pain in my tummy, the kind of dragging I usually felt before a period.

Hope flickered for a second but I squashed it, it couldn't be, but it could . . . No, it couldn't . . . The doctor had agreed with me that I was pregnant. But he could have made a mistake, he was very old, he hadn't even examined me. The pain persisted and then, just before the eleven o'clock tea break, it happened . . . my period started to come.

At first I pretended to ignore it, but then it started to get heavier. I'd be destroyed, I had nothing on but light knickers but I didn't care. It was coming, it was coming, it was coming . . . I wasn't pregnant after all, that silly old doctor pretending to know everything, he's a fool, he's a fool . . . thanks, God, thanks, thanks,

thanks, I'm not pregnant. I danced around my tiny office, I noticed the trees outside my window were beginning to put out the faintest buds, the world was wonderful, I'd never go near a man again, I'd be a virgin for the rest of my life, the relief. I could never survive a fright like that again, never, never, never . . .

Christ, my doctor was very bad really, pretending he knew I was pregnant, when he hadn't a clue, saying such dreadful things about Eric. Fucking hell, it wasn't good enough, I'd give him a piece of my mind tomorrow night, daft auld thing . . . It was true what people said about him after all, he was as crazy as a coot. In a way I had inherited him with the flat. He had been Edith's doctor for most of her life and she was always singing his praises. Once, shortly after I came to live here I had spent the night in agony with pains in my tummy and in my back. For two years since I came to Dublin I had been having these pains. I had seen several specialists, had had all kinds of tests and X-rays, but nobody could find a reason for them. One minute I'd be fine and the next doubled up in agony. This had been one of the worst nights I had spent and at about seven o'clock in the morning Edith had rung 'D'Arcy' as she always called him; she never used his first name or called him 'doctor'.

He arrived almost immediately, a huge big man, at that time in his early seventies, but looking about fifty. Edith used always say that as a young man he was frightfully attractive, and I could well believe her. That morning however I was lying on the bed with barely the energy to tell him how I felt and all he did was stand looking out the window, making a big speech about the beauty of the garden. I remember thinking, 'Christ almighty, here I am dying on the bed and Edith would have to get this mad quack for me.'

He went away and half an hour later he was back with two pills. I took them and the pain went away and it never came back. From then on he could do no wrong in my eyes. I soon realised there were two schools of thought on D'Arcy — those who swore by him and those who swore against him; there was no in between. I was now beginning to join the latter camp. I'd go to him all right tomorrow night, but it would be to give him a bit of my mind.

Jesus, while I was dreaming my period was getting really heavy. I must go down and find something to put on quick. My office was the annexe on the turn of the stairs from the first floor down to the basement, where the toilets were. I skipped down the stairs and met my boss half way up. Normally we glared at each other in mutual detestation, but now as he stood back to let me pass I gave him my most brilliant smile and friendly greeting. He didn't know how to react, he looked as if his world had suddenly fallen apart. I giggled in devilment as I locked the toilet door and pulled down my knickers . . . There was no blood, no blood . . . there was a very heavy discharge but no blood. Oh God! How could You be so cruel . . . I had been so sure I had my period, now the black desolation was back again. I sat down on the toilet seat and cried and cried . . .

The doctor opened the door the instant I rang the bell. He had his overcoat on, ready to go out on a call.

'Well, your test was positive, child, you are pregnant all right.'

I barely nodded, I felt completely dead and drained, it didn't seem to me to be particularly interesting whether or not I was pregnant.

'Are you all right?' he asked and I could feel that he was anxious about me.

'Yes, yes, I'm grand — I'll be fine.'

'I've got to go out on a call now, but I'll be back in an hour. Ring me if you need me. Look, go home now and smoke twenty fags.'

By this time we had both reached the street and were separating in different directions.

'Yes doctor, I'll do that, I'll be all right. 'Bye, and thanks.'

I wandered back to the flat and slumped into a chair

in front of the television. I took out the fags and nearly smiled at the advice I had just been given. I felt sure it must be most unorthodox advice for a doctor to give a pregnant woman and yet it was OK. He was forcing me to be calm, to realise that my problem was only one of many he had to deal with every day. Strange, there was no sympathy in him at all, just plain ordinary kindness. That I supposed was why I liked him so much. I agreed with Wilde when he said 'Damn sympathy, there is too much of that kind of thing in the world.' Sympathy in operation it seemed to me was an external expression such as 'oh you poor thing! Oh isn't that awful! Oh how very sad!' — and so on, completely dissociating the person from any responsibility for the other person's dilemma. Kindness, on the other hand, was a practical realisation that we are all in some way or another responsible for each other's problems, and must help in whatever way we can.

I wandered around the flat. So I *was* pregnant, I *was* going to have a baby. Funny, now I didn't feel a thing, not a thing. I'll tell you what — I made a pact with myself — forget all about it for a week or so, there is nothing you can do about it for the moment, so you might as well try to relax and enjoy yourself. That seemed like a good idea. I owed lots of social calls, I hadn't been out with any of my women friends for ages, I wanted to take Edith out. I'd get cracking, tonight I'd wash my hair, tomorrow I'd be ready for action.

VIII

It worked. I rang up one of the girls and we went to a show at the Gate; a crowd of us went to a ballad session out in the Old Shieling; I took Edith out to a film; I visited friends all over town; I avoided Betty, she would want to ask me questions I didn't want to answer. It was great, I was having a fine time, to hell with all this pregnancy bit, I didn't care. I kept it up for nearly two weeks.

One day at the office the girls were talking about going dancing at the Met that night. I said I'd come along. I hadn't been there for ages. The Metropole was an institution in Dublin. It was said that sooner or later everyone turned up there. Half way up O'Connell Street, it was a fine old building, with a big cinema on the ground floor and bars and restaurants and a fine dance hall on the second floor. The dance hall was lovely. The floor was fairly small and was surrounded on three sides by balconies where you could sit and have coffee or drinks and watch the passing parade. One was never too old or too young for the Met. They were there from nineteen to ninety, positive proof that hope springs eternal in the human breast. It was supposed to be full of married men out on the tear, but sure that didn't matter, you could smell a married man a mile away.

We were not being asked to dance very much that night and we were sitting on one of the balconies having coffee and watching the antics of a pair out on the floor. Suddenly

I was looking down straight into Eric's face. He was dancing in the middle of the floor, wrapped around a woman and obviously ready to get up on her given half the chance. I didn't believe it — the barriers I had erected in the past fortnight came crashing down around me. I was sitting there in the Met, pregnant, unmarried, and the father of my child was dancing in front of my eyes with another woman, looking through me and pretending I wasn't there. Just then one of the women said:

'Hey, there's Eric!'

Oh, fucking hell, that did it. I couldn't bear it. 'I'm going home.' I was half way out the door already. Joan followed me. We didn't talk much on the way home. Joan knew there was something wrong between Eric and me and that I'd talk about it in my own good time. There was a lot of support and understanding between the crowd of us, as our various love lives unwound their sometimes tortuous courses. Would the same support apply, I wondered, if the girls knew my real situation? I dropped Joan at her own home and then sat in the car outside my flat. Eric's car wasn't back yet, did that mean — oh — it couldn't — he couldn't be taking that woman home!

'Of course he could, you little fool. Not only could he take her home, but he could be fucking her right now. What do you think of that?'

Eric's car drew up outside his own door, he went into the house without ever even looking in my direction. I sat there with the tears running down my face like a cur that has been whipped by its owner.

* * *

The next evening I came straight home from work. I had sworn I'd make a plan, but where in hell's name was I supposed to start? I sat down with the packet of fags to try and think. I must somehow or another get it into my head that I was going to have a baby and I must figure out how to survive these nine months. Not even nine months now, I was about ten weeks gone, so only about seven months more. I must get a book on pregnancy. I hadn't a clue about what being pregnant actually involved.

I must also leave the flat, that was obvious. I knew I could tell Edith and she would insist on my staying, but I also knew it would involve conflict with other people in the house and I couldn't cause her distress. I'd have to start dropping hints to her that I'd be leaving, think up some good excuse. I'd get a flat easily enough, I felt sure, there were always lots of them advertised in the *Evening Press*. I'd need to move out before the end of April, before anyone spotted my condition. That would give me plenty of time to find a good flat. I'd also have to keep my job, which meant they mustn't find out I was pregnant in the office. 'They' in particular meant my boss. In his own mind he was the greatest liberal of the century, but I knew if he found out about me my life would be a misery. He might even find an excuse to sack me anyway. No, I must keep it a secret. If I didn't have a job I was finished altogether. One of the things to do was to get into the office before nine o'clock in the morning. If I could do that, then I could sneak in and up the back stairs and nobody would spot me.

I'd also have to tell Susan and Joan. How would they react, would they desert me? I decided not to think about it. I'd have to have some support, so I'd just have to tell them and let them like it or lump it. Christ, that sounded much braver than I felt.

Straight away I put my plan into operation. I was in the office next morning at five to nine. And the next, and the next, and the next. At first the expressions on the faces of people who came in to leave things on my desk and found me there were hilarious. The first morning they just thought that I had been out at an all-night party and come straight on. The next morning it was more serious.

'Ah, so you've turned over a new leaf?'

'Practising for entering a convent?'

'It must be the change before the death!'

By the fourth morning they had forgotten that I was ever late for work in my life.

One day I sneaked into Easons to buy a book on pregnancy. I grabbed the first one I saw and felt like a criminal as I took it to the cash desk under several others that I had bought but didn't want. One always met someone one knew in Easons, it was that kind of place — what if I met a friend and they saw me with a book on pregnancy? At last I got out of the place without seeing a face I knew.

The minute I got home that night I took it out. On the cover was a beautiful woman, with a soft, gentle face, wearing a soft, gentle smile, with soft gently waving hair. She stood in a soft, flowing gown, looking out on a soft, well-tended garden. She was softly, gently pregnant. The first page assured me that to be pregnant was the most wonderful thing in the world, that a woman was at her most beautiful, that it was a time of calmness and serenity.

Jesus Christ, who was I then? Here I was in a state of misery, wishing to God I wasn't pregnant and I had to read this bilge. At six weeks a woman could expect to suffer from morning sickness, it went on. This could take the form of nausea and vomiting, but not to worry, if a woman sat up slowly when she woke and her husband brought her a nice cup of weak tea and a biscuit and she rested in bed, it wouldn't be so bad. As long as a woman felt loved and cherished by her husband, pregnancy was a time of contentment and joy and total fulfilment.

Ah, fucking hell. Here I was without a man in the world to love me, let alone a husband. Was I the only woman then who didn't have a man around to be bringing me cups of tea and cherishing me when I was pregnant? Or who were these bloody books written for? And the morning sickness, of course I'd heard of that, who hadn't? It was the bane of every pregnant woman's life. That would finish me, there was no way I could be getting sick in the office every morning without someone spotting me. I'd never manage to stay in the office and not be found out. I'd have to think of something else. There must be someone who could help me, but who, where? Surely there was another unmarried mother somewhere. What about Edith's woman up the road? Maybe she could tell me what to do.

'Oh yeah, that would be great. You could go up and knock on her door and say "excuse me, Miss . . . er am . . . Mrs . . . ah Madam? I believe you had a son thirty or thirty-five years ago and your father put you out in the snow, but you kept the baby and he is doing very well for himself now, would you please tell me how you did it?" Yes that's it, that would be marvellous, go on up now and say all that to a woman you've never seen, let alone met, and she'll be delighted with you. She'll give you all the answers, steps one, two and three, on how to survive in Ireland when you are pregnant and not married. I'll tell you how she managed, because she probably had some guts, a few brains, a bit of imagination and she got on with it.'

I remembered seeing something about unmarried mothers in the small ads in the *Evening Press*. I was fascinated by the small ads and often spent hours reading them. You could find anything you wanted there. I searched now with excitement and sure enough, there it was under *Miscellaneous* — 'The Catholic Protection and Rescue Society, South Anne Street.' Good suffering Jesus, who were the Catholic Protection and Rescue Society and who did they rescue and protect? What kind of weird people hid behind a name like that? Oh no, I might be at the bottom of the barrel, but I neither wanted to be rescued nor protected, all I wanted was someone to talk to, someone who could help me to sort out the jumble of mad thoughts that substituted for my mind just now. But who were the people who could help me? It was stupid that I had to be in this state because I was pregnant and had no husband, but if I got married in the morning, everything would be all right. It wouldn't matter if I hated the man I married and reared a child in the atmosphere that would create, as long as the conventions were observed.

For as long as I could remember the worst thing that could happen to anyone's daughter in Ireland was to have a baby and not be married. Not that it was ever spelled out by my parents. Sex was never mentioned in our house. Neither for that matter was love. Like lots of people in my age group I was never told the 'facts of life' and the terror of my first period was still vivid in my mind, being in school with no protection but a pair of knickers, and a pretty worn pair at that, and the discomfort and the odour and the feeling that one had committed some dreadful sin. Because I was younger than most of my pals, the information which was gathered by the group was not always passed on to me.

It was as a great favour, in fact, that I was allowed to come to the secret demonstration, by one of the older girls, of how babies were actually made.

IX

The Gaelic Athletic Association park was about a mile outside our small town. It was several acres of playing fields and it was here that the noble games of hurling, football and camogie were played. Because this was the time when the 'Ban' on foreign games still operated, the people who played rugby or soccer had to do so in a muddy field miles away where they wouldn't be a bad example to the rest of us. There was a lovely little wood of fir trees at one end of the field and it was here one afternoon after school, that we met in giggling excitement to be initiated into the strange antics of grown-ups.

The girl who had all this breathtaking knowledge was at least five years older than me and slept in the same room as her parents. They had only one room anyway and everybody slept in it, and it was thus that she became the undisputed authority on how babies are made.

We crawled as far as we could into the wood, and amid much half guilty whispering, we were told to take off our knickers and lie down on the pine needles. It was lovely lying there in our bare bums, on the thick dry pine needles, in the green semi-darkness, secure from all prying adult eyes and able to get on with our proper education. Our leader explained to us that her father climbed up on her mother in the bed and put his thing into her wee-wee, and kinda rode up and down on her somehow, like you'd do on a horse, and there would be lots of grunting and groaning and sometimes her mother would shout:

'Ye fuckin' eejit, don't stay in there too long.'

Of course we all knew that men had things that we didn't have, though none of us had ever seen one except the girl who was teaching us. Since she didn't have one, she lay on top of each of us in turn, rubbing her wee-wee against ours. She had much more hair than the rest of us and it was very tickly and funny. Then we did it to each other and examined each other and discovered we had tiny little things and if we rubbed them together it gave us a lovely tingly feeling. We also discovered that if one sat on the other's bum while she was doing it to a third, it made it even better, lent it a bit of weight or something. We practiced on each other until we got tired, then sat around wondering about the strange antics of grown ups. Several of us felt sure that the man must put his thing into the woman's belly button, because it was obvious that that was what it was for. Not even our knowledgeable friend could tell us how babies were supposed to come out through such tiny holes and we began to have grave doubts about these 'facts of life'. Whenever I saw my friend's parents after that I gazed at them in wonder, trying to visualise them in bed making babies. The more I looked at them the more I decided it couldn't happen the way my friend described. He was an enormous man with a huge belly and no teeth. She was a tiny little woman with cropped grey hair and a leathery face. She wore dispensary glasses and never washed herself.

It was at this kind of session that we learned about sex, and here also we began to understand that the greatest sin for a girl was to have a baby without being married. Nobody ever knew who said it, or where the information came from, but the frightened whispers went from one to the other of us. We told each other vague stories, after crossing our hearts and hoping to die if we weren't telling the truth, of girls who went to England and never came back.

For a long time I carried my guilty knowledge around with me, while pretending to be innocent, and then one day I knew that my parents knew that I knew the 'facts of life'. How were we supposed to have found out? I've often wondered since. There were no books one could get to read in a small town in Ireland in those days. The worst thing to be found was the loathsome *News of the World*, which was brought in from England by very bad people. It was written by Satan himself and those who read it went straight to hell. I think the beginning of the end of my association with the Catholic Church came when I discovered that the President of our junior presidium of the Legion of Mary read the *News of the World*; not only did she not go to hell immediately, but she continued to be our President.

She was the mother of one of my friends and every week she sent us with a message to one of her friends. One day the message wasn't very well wrapped up and we decided to open it. Our eyes nearly fell out when we saw the dreaded newspaper. We were half way down the Main Street, and we sat down in a shop doorway to try and read it. There seemed to be lots about rape and murder, but one thing was for sure, it wasn't written by Satan at all, the names of the people who wrote it were across the front page, just like you'd get on a paper in Ireland. We wrapped it up again as best we could and delivered it. We never spoke about it again but a large chunk of faith had been chopped away. After that I began to take the priests with a grain of salt, and the Legion of Mary too. They had a lot to be responsible for.

'Well, they're not responsible for your present predicament. You can't blame this on your parents or priests or nuns or the Legion, or anyone but yourself. It's a long time now, me girl, since you didn't know what sex was all about. This is Dublin 1970, and you're thirty years of age. You're pregnant because you went to bed with a man and had sex without taking precautions. So stop sitting there feeling all sorry for yourself because nobody told you about babies when you were twelve or thirteen.'

'Did I blame anyone? All I'm saying is that there is something wrong with this shagging country, when I feel like a criminal because I'm pregnant and the only people I can find to help me are called The Catholic Protection and Rescue Society.'

'Why doesn't the father of your child help you?'

Where was Eric? I hadn't seen him since the night at the Met. How was it that one day we were madly in love and all involved in each other's affairs, and then we were apart, not interested in each other, not seeing each other? And yet we had never discussed it, never talked about breaking up, it was as if we played a game by some unspecified rules which we both clearly understood. But Eric was the father of my unborn child. It was his business, he had to help me, I'd go and see him.

He lived in one of those luxury flats where the door is opened by remote control. He knew my signal, two shorts and a long jab on the bell. He came bounding down the stairs to meet me, threw his arms around me and practically carried me up to the flat, sat me down and poured me a huge brandy, all the time talking as if he was about to run out of breath.

'Oh my love, you're back, I've missed you so much, was it bad? are you better? I'm so glad it is all over . . . ' meantime pawing me and slobbering all over me.

I sat staring at him as if he was some kind of strange specimen that needed careful studying before making any decision about it. I decided someone in the room was gone stone daft and it wasn't me. What was this bloody fucker going on about? The last time I'd seen him he had pretended he didn't even see me. He hadn't come near me since he knew I was pregnant, he hadn't given two damns what happened to me, yet here he was trying to ease me into a position where his big prick could make contact. I nearly spat at him as I pushed him away from me.

'Eric, what are you talking about, is what over?'

'The abortion! You've had the abortion?'

I'd been through so much since, I had forgotten that the last he'd heard was that I was going to have an abortion. So the bastard thought it was all over and there were no more problems and he was ready to ride me again.

'No, Eric. I haven't had an abortion. I'm not going to have one. I'm going to have our baby. You will help me, won't you?'

He had changed again now, all the ardour was gone, he moved away from me fiddling around the room with the record player, his face gone all cold and cagey looking.

'I don't know how I can help you.'

'Well, at least you can give me some money.'

'What for?'

'Oh for heaven's sake, for the hospital, for baby things, I don't know, but I must have it.'

'What kind of things do you want for the baby?'

'Jesus Christ!' My patience was running out fast. 'The kind of things babies need — food, clothes, carry cot, bottles — all those kind of things.'

'You don't intend keeping the baby? Surely that's not what you are thinking of doing!'

'Of course I can keep it, what do you think I'm going to do? Give it away? It's my baby.' We were confronting each other now, glaring at each other, and on Eric's face there was a look of complete panic.

'You can't keep that baby, you've got to have it adopted.'

'I will not, I will not!' My voice was beginning to rise hysterically. 'I will not have my child adopted, I will not give it away to be reared by somebody else, do you understand that? I'll rear my own child.' The tears were beginning but I pushed them away. If I was going to have to fight so hard, then the time for tears was over. I glared at Eric, waiting for the next onslaught.

But then as quickly he changed again. 'It's all right, you can keep your baby, I'll help you.' He put his arms around me and soothed me.

'Trust me, I'll help you . . .' Meantime he was moving me backwards, stroking my hair and crooning to me. I felt as though I was standing at the other end of the room, watching this scene with total detachment. Eric eased me on to the bed and spread my legs wide. Then kneeling on the floor he pulled my bottom towards the edge of the bed until his big cock rested on my fanny. I could feel it through his trousers like an iron bar. I lay there completely unmoved, thinking a block of wood would have more effect on me, but pressing myself gently against him.

I knew that in a few seconds the prick would be out of the trousers and up my fanny, so without appearing to hurry I eased my foot out of my shoe and brought my knee up towards my chest, then placed my stockinged foot over his balls and prick, rubbing my big toe around the top of his cock which was ready to burst. I kept up the pressure until he had fallen back on his hands with his eyes closed in a state of drooling ecstasy.

And then I kicked. With my left shod foot I kicked as hard as I could straight into his balls. The look of terror and bewilderment on his face was the last thing I saw as I made off out the door and down the stairs. That will put a halt to his gallop for a while, I thought, with a rush of pure hatred, as I went back to my own flat.

Had anyone told me that such a scene could take place I would never have believed them. All Eric wanted to do was fuck, while I was up to my neck in trouble, and a baby was going to be born that would have no father and would be called illegitimate. Oh, Christ! Neither would I have believed that Eric could mean so little to me. I was both sad and elated when I thought that I was probably finished with men.

My sex life was over. Ah well, it had been good while it lasted. I could never imagine letting a man lay a finger on me. Never again.

PART TWO

X

I was sick — God was I sick! I woke to my usual desolate misery and on top of that was the awful feeling of nausea in my belly, rising up into my mouth. So the bloody book was right, this was morning sickness. I thought it had said that the sickness started at six weeks. I must be nearly twelve by now. 'Lie quietly', said the book, 'until your husband brings you a nice cup of weak tea.'

I lay there trying to breathe slowly and deeply.

'You fuckin' eejit, are you going to lie there for the rest of your life waiting for a husband to bring you tea? Don't you know you've no husband? Or do you think that damned book is going to produce one for you?' I was going to vomit. I staggered out to the loo. I didn't get sick, but I felt sure I was going to any minute. Maybe if I made myself a cup of weak tea and brought it in to myself in bed, that might do the trick. I could never see the point of spoiling good water with a few leaves of tea, but weak tea the book said, so that's what I made. I felt like a half fool sitting up in bed sipping shamrock tea (three leaves to the pot) and nibbling my dainty little biscuit.

However, it seemed to be working, the nausea did seem to be subsiding a little.

I lay there until a quarter past eight and then got out of bed as if I was made of thistledown. I dressed slowly, brushed my teeth slowly, drank another slow cup of weak tea. By the time I was ready to go out the door I felt old. My usual routine — out of bed, into clothes, wash teeth, out the door, into the car — took about seven minutes. This morning it had taken the best part of forty minutes. Nevertheless if it kept me from puking all over the office I supposed it was worth it. I was in before nine, which no longer caused any comment. On the contrary, I was now the paragon who was first in and last out of the office. Strange how reputations are made, I thought.

For two more mornings I went through the same rig-marole, waking up dying, sipping the witch's piss, crawling into work. On the fourth morning sitting up in bed sipping the brew, it suddenly struck me that I wasn't sick at all.

I leaped out of bed, sat down on the edge and lit a fag. Jesus, I had believed I was sick because the bloody book had said it. I probably had felt a bit bad on that first morning and had exaggerated it because that was the way the book suggested I feel. People who wrote books like that should be put in jail! Had it said there was a possibility that one might be sick in the morning? Oh no, it was certain that one would be sick, and that all nice sick, pregnant women would have nice attentive husbands on hand to bring them nice cups of weak tea. What about all the widows whose children were born after their husbands died? What about all the women whose husbands had left them? God Almighty! Didn't I have lots of friends with the best husbands in the world, who were nevertheless away when their wives were in labour? Who was the bloody book aimed at then? I caught it and with all my strength flung it at the far wall of the room. For good measure I threw the cup of nice weak tea after it. The cup flew into smithereens against the wall. I felt much better. I wasn't sick. Please God I wasn't going to be sick. Maybe that was nature's compensation. Maybe nature thought it a bit daft to be giving women with no husbands morning sickness.

That was the end of that episode. I began to feel better. Things would work out all right. If I just made my plans and worked step by step, maybe I'd get away with it.

A flat was my next problem. I must try to be moved out by the middle of April before I began to show. Once or twice recently I had hinted to Edith that I'd be leaving the flat. I knew she was terribly hurt and felt it had something to do with her. I told her that a lot of my friends were coming up from the country and that we wanted to get a big flat together. I tried to assure her that I'd be around and would call her and still bring her out. That I'd find somebody else to take the flat. Inside me I was tormented at the pain I was causing her, yet I couldn't think of any other way of dealing with the situation.

Poor Edith. I pretended to be very flippant with her, and a bit brusque. I assured her that it was not the end of the world, that whoever came after me would probably be much easier to live with, that a change was good, that she would have more friends than ever. All the time I just wanted to put my head on her lap and cry.

Another problem was telling Susan and Joan. I wanted to tell them because not only did I need their help but I hated keeping such a secret from them. Every morning and afternoon they had their tea-breaks in my office. Sometimes these breaks stretched to half an hour, much to the annoyance of our boss and his male cronies, who seemed to be convinced that we spent our time talking about them, or plotting against them. This both irritated and amused me. In fact we couldn't care less about what they did, we were obviously far less interested in their carry-on than they were in ours. They seemed to take it as a personal affront that the women should get together.

One morning Susan was in first and before I had time to think about it I said it.

'Susan, I'm pregnant!' I nearly burst holding my breath waiting for her reaction. She said,

'Oh dear.' That seemed to be the end of the conversation. I looked at her to see if there was any disapproval, any disdain. There was none evident in her face. In a way Susan lived a rather protected life, at home with her parents and two sisters. She had two brothers married and living in Dublin and one married in England. She was a very good

Catholic, went to Mass during the week, devotions, and First Fridays and she constantly reprimanded me for my appalling language. Now I was to find out her true worth.

After a while she asked, 'What are your plans?'

I poured it all out, my intention of keeping the baby, of wanting to change flats, of the need to work for as long as possible because I'd have to have money. She agreed that if the boss ever found out I was finished, and the biggest bogey was Richard, who had a nose for secrets worse than a ferret for a rabbit, and couldn't keep a bit of information to himself to save his life. We would have to be careful of Richard. Susan was the boss's private secretary and her office was upstairs, just outside his. She would be able to keep tabs on him.

'I can't see how you are going to manage the way you think you are,' Susan said, 'but any help you want I'll give, and I have some money which you can have.' I had to choke down the tears and the gratitude. Here was help offered without any advice, or argument, or questions.

'Have you told Joan yet?'

'No, but I must. I'll tell her tonight, we'll need her help.'

Suddenly Susan burst out laughing. 'So that's why you've been coming in before nine in the morning. There's no doubt about it, you're a cute one . . . '

'Come and have tea with me', I said to Joan as I drove her home that evening. We often did this. Joan also lived at home with her parents and a brother, and I'd go to her house or Susan's for my tea, or they would come to the flat, depending on which was most convenient for what we were doing in the evening. I loved going to their houses because their mothers insisted on feeding me properly, as they said, with their lovely home cooking. I always told them that I cooked my food at home too, but that was all that could be said for it.

'I've something to tell you,' I said to her as we sat having our tea. 'I'm pregnant.'

'Ah, I thought as much,' was her unexpected reply.

'What do you mean, you thought as much?' It seemed

to me that the only person to be surprised by my being pregnant was me.

'Because you've been very strange and uneasy lately, and I knew there was something wrong with you. What are you going to do?' Again I told all my plans.

But it wasn't as easy with Joan. 'Who's the father?' she asked. Somehow I resented that question and didn't want to answer it.

'Never mind the father, Joan,' I tried to parry her.

'But it's Eric, isn't it? Why on earth don't you want to tell me?'

'Because I don't, now stop tormenting me!'

'Oh, all right.' She was obviously very offended, but I couldn't help it. 'What are you going to do with the baby?'

'I'm going to keep it, of course, what do you expect me to do with it?'

'You could have it adopted. It's not fair to keep a child on your own. How will you manage? Who'll mind it? You can't mind a child and work at the same time. And it will have no father. What kind of life can you give a child?'

I had to clench my teeth to stop myself screaming. 'Look, Joan, just help me to survive until the baby arrives, I can't think beyond that. If I can have the baby and hold on to my job, somehow I'll manage.'

'You'll never manage to keep it a secret in the office.'

'But we can try, Joan, and with you and Susan helping, I should be able to get away with it well into June, or even July, and then I'll have to think of something else.'

'You know I'll give you all the help I can, it's just that you seem to be making difficulties for yourself. Now if you went away to England for a year and had the baby there, you could easily say you were married and then come back. I'd even go with you, I could do with a change of scene.' Joan was clearly puzzled as to why I wouldn't clear out and be done with it, and in a way so was I. It would be so much less complicated just to disappear for a year or two . . . but this was my country and I wanted to stay in it, and I wanted my baby to be born here. Maybe I'd go away then . . . 'The thing is that there are no unmarried mothers rearing their children here.' Joan broke into my thoughts.

'There are, Joan, there are, I'm telling you we've just got to find them. It is nonsense to think that every woman who gets pregnant without being married either leaves the country or has her child adopted. I don't believe it.' I told Joan about Edith's woman up the road. Strange that this woman whom I'd never seen was my main source of strength at the moment. 'If she could keep her child and rear him on her own, all those years ago, then by God I'll have a good shot at doing it now.'

XI

The next evening I went through the *Evening Press* and picked out a few flats that were not too far away and seemed reasonable. They were all on view between six and eight and I thought I'd have a look at them on the way to Betty's.

The first one had three or four people already standing around waiting to see it.

I couldn't be bothered with that lark so I went on to the next one. It was gone and so were the other two. They were all I had picked out. I decided that they must have been in the paper for three or four nights and that I would try again the next day.

At first Betty was amazed that I should be considering keeping the baby, but then she agreed that it was the most natural thing to do. Her husband had died tragically when her children were very young and she had reared four of them on her own, with very little money and a lot of hardship in the early years. Her one advantage was that she had owned her own house. Now things were beginning to be a little easier for her, the children were growing up, she had found herself a fairly good job, and had managed to buy herself a car. So she could see no reason why I couldn't rear one child.

'You've got a good salary and you should be able to stay in the job until about June with a bit of luck.'

'Betty, I've got to stay in this job until the very end.

The baby isn't due until September, what would I do in the meantime? I've got to have a decent flat, to have some-place to bring the baby and if I lose this job, who the hell is going to employ me at six months pregnant? As well as that, I'm entitled to six weeks sick leave on full pay and three weeks holidays on this job, so if I can stay there until the middle of August then I'm away in a hack.'

'Oh we'll see . . . ' Betty sighed. 'You are just the kind of bitch who would get away with it. Anyway you can always stay here, you know that.'

'I know, but don't you understand, I must provide a home for my child, I can't have my baby living on charity just because I can't provide for it. Isn't it strange, we'll both be in the same situation, rearing children on our own, but because you've got a marriage certificate and a photo-graph up on the wall that you can point to, or because you can take the kids out to Glasnevin and point to a slab and say 'there's your Da', you've somehow got acceptance and respectability. None of your children remember Paul, do they? But he was there and you were married and it was all proper and correct. What will I tell my poor child about its father? What will I show it?'

Oh God, the depression was coming down on top of me again. Maybe I should have had that abortion, maybe I shouldn't be trying to keep my baby. What was I letting the child in for? It was one thing to have me in a misery, but was I letting an innocent child in for a life of derision and contempt, always deprived because I didn't marry its father? Maybe I should have it adopted, give it away when it was born for somebody else to rear. Would that solve the child's problem? It would certainly solve mine, all I would have to bear would be the pain. But what about the child? Sooner or later it would find out that it was adopted and what then? Where would it look for its background, who would tell it about its mother? How would it be made to understand that I hadn't really rejected it? That it was circumstances which had made me give it away to some-body else?

'What on earth are you crying for?' Betty broke into my

thoughts. I didn't even know that I had been crying, but the tears were streaming down my face.

'I can't give away my baby, Betty,' I wailed at her, 'I can't.'

'Aren't you the awful eejit altogether,' she said, 'to be carrying on with that nonsense. Nobody is asking you to give away your baby, you will be able to keep it and everything will turn out all right, you'll see. Anyway do you want a boy or a girl?'

'A what?' I stuttered at her.

'A boy or a girl, ye fool, do you realise that you are going to have a son or a daughter, though knowing you, God knows what you'll have.'

Good lord, I hadn't thought about it. Before the end of the year I'd have a son or a daughter. I couldn't imagine it.

My spirits had revived again by the time I was leaving Betty's. I promised her I'd ring the minute I found a flat, which I expected to in the next few days . . .

Every evening that week I went through the *Evening Press* and picked out three or four flats. Every evening was a repetition of the first one. By the time I got there the place was already gone, or there was a big line of people in front of me. I nearly died of shock when I saw some of the places that were advertised. All around the Ballsbridge area, old elegant houses had been converted into modern self-contained bedsits. They were a nightmare. Beautiful old rooms had been divided two or three times into dreary cubbyholes. Granted they had all the 'mod cons', but Jesus fucking Christ, you couldn't swing a cat in them, let alone rear a child. They were usually double the price of my present flat. What would I do? By the end of the first week I was in a panic, by the middle of the second I was in despair. I had told Edith that my friends were coming up and that I would be ready to move around the middle of April. It was then the last week in March.

Susan and Joan said they'd help me. We started getting the paper in the office in the early afternoon and trying to eliminate the places that were already gone by phone. The minute it was five o'clock we chased out of the office and straight to the first address. We'd still be at it at eight o'clock at night, frozen and hungry and weary. The weather was bitter and our feet were worn up to our knees, trudging from one end of the city to the other. We saw flats of all shapes and sizes, some with bathrooms, some with only one toilet for about four or five tenants. Some with cookers on the landing, some with cookers practically sitting on the bed. Any I thought suitable were about three times what I could afford, and any I could afford and were offered to me had a landlord built in and that was no good. Joan and Susan were fed up. I knew they felt I should take some bloody place for the moment, and then when the weather got warmer and the students went home it might be easier to find someplace else. The strain became unbearable. We hardly spoke to each other as we did the rounds every evening.

One afternoon when I was going through the paper as usual I came across an ad: 'Two roomed flat to let, £3 per week, contact caretaker.' Christ, only three pounds for two rooms, if only I could get it and with a caretaker and all it must be fairly OK. At a quarter to five Joan and I left the office and we found the address easily enough. It was in Wolfe Square and as we drove into it we were quite impressed. It was a lovely little square of two storied terraced houses, with two or three steps up to the front doors and railings in front of each house. They were all brightly painted and well kept. My spirits rose. As we drove down the left hand side of the square looking for the number, it became obvious that it must be one of the two houses facing us on the angle of the square. We came to a stop in front of them. Both our faces, I knew, were registering the same look of disbelief. Without saying a word to each other we got out of the car and stood gaping. It was the classical slum scene, which I had read about a hundred times but never seen so clearly before. Structurally the houses were the same as all the others, but there it ended. The paintwork was nonexistent, the windows were filthy. Some of them had raggedy bits of curtains, others had nothing at all. There were two or three bins outside each door stuffed with rubbish, spilling down the steps and onto the pavements. A cat sat on top of one of the bins washing itself as meticulously as if it were sitting on a Persian carpet. We took a few steps closer to make sure of the number and realised that there was a card on the door which indicated somebody was dead in the house. With relief we decided that you couldn't go knocking on a door with somebody dead in the house. We were just turning away when the door opened and a pan of water was flung straight out onto the pavement. We stumbled back, barely missing a drenching. Then a woman appeared holding a pan.

'Ah did I nearly drownd the two of yez, God love yez,' she roared at us energetically.

We stared at her, the cat glared at her. She managed to stare at us and glare at the cat at the same time.

'Is it about the rooms yez are come?' she queried. I nodded, and then feeling my voice might work, whispered,

'We didn't like to knock on account of the death in the house.'

'Ah never mind that, sure people die every day,' she said, obviously appreciating the fact that it hadn't come to her turn yet.

'G'wan in there next door now, to Mr. Mullins, he's the caretaker like, an' he'll look after yez.'

'Go on in,' Joan was muttering out of the corner of her mouth. 'Maybe it's not as bad as it looks, you can always clean it up. Think of the cheap rent, and nobody would ever find you here.'

The woman was still standing outside her door, waiting, determined not to move until I found Mr. Mullins. I went up the steps to the other door. It was wide open and the stench that came out didn't hit you, it wrapped itself around you and squeezed the life out of you. I gasped for breath and turned to run when there was a creak on the right hand side of the hall. It was obviously a door opening, but I could see nothing in the filthy gloom, and then there was an old woman standing in front of me

73

as if she had appeared out of a bottle.

'It'll be Mr. Mullins yez'll be looking for,' she croaked at me. 'Go down the stairs now and knock at the white door at the bottom,' she wheezed. 'He's there all right.'

I passed by her into the hall, trying hard not to breathe and went straight on to where I figured the stairs must lead down to the basement. I put out my foot in an act of faith, there was no way of seeing, it was just pitch blackness. I felt with the back of my heel, one step after another, each time feeling I was stepping out into space. In fact there could only have been about ten steps, but it took me several minutes to get down. I stood in the darkness at the bottom, terrified. I couldn't move. If I stretched my arms out to feel my way, something slimy would surely grab me. I was certain all kinds of things were creeping and writhing around my feet. The stench was choking me. The bile was coming up into my mouth and any minute I was going to retch.

'Knock on the white door!' the hag was screeching from above. 'Knock loud, he's a bit deaf, he wears a peaked cap.' What white door? There wasn't any door, there was nothing but pitch blackness.

'Did he answer ye? Knock loud, on the white door . . . '

I must have gone mad, and someone had put me in an asylum. I rushed up the stairs and out to the car. Joan was already sitting in it. I tried to get the key in the ignition but couldn't manage it because I was shaking so much. Joan lit a cigarette and handed it to me. I sat hanging on to the steering wheel until the shaking stopped. Then I turned the car to drive out of the square. The two women were still standing on the steps looking at us.

'He's very deaf, he wears a peaked cap, you'll know him . . . ' the old woman was still croaking at us. Then the two of them turned and went back into the houses.

I drove Joan home. She wanted me to come in but I couldn't face anyone. I went home and slumped in a chair, completely drained.

So this is what looking for a flat in Dublin was all about. Often, friends had commented on how lucky I was to have such a lovely place so cheap. I had never paid too much attention to them, but then I had never had to look for a flat in Dublin. When I came up from the country a friend of mine was moving out of Edith's to get married, and I just moved in.

If it was that difficult for a single person to get somewhere to live, what would it be like for one who was obviously pregnant, or had a child?

XII

Edith knocked and came hobbling in full of excitement. Edith at seventy-six could dance all night, but she could hardly walk at all. She was very bad on the feet, they were full of warts and bunions and corns and she was tormented with them.

'Great news,' she warbled in her Ascendancy voice. 'Deirdre is taking the flat.'

'Oh Edith,' I sprang up and gave her a big hug, 'I knew that it would work out all right, aren't you delighted?' I was so glad; the fact that Deirdre was coming eased my own guilt at deserting Edith. She was another friend of Mabel's from whom I had inherited the place. She was full of life and good humour and she would be great for Edith.

'Of course,' Edith was saying in her usual diplomatic way, 'there will never be anyone as nice as you . . . '

'Oh come on Edith,' I kidded her, 'things will be better than ever. Think of it, now you'll have Mabel and Deirdre and me to take you out. I won't be that far away and we'll go out as much as ever.' That, I felt sure, was a lie. Still maybe I could come for some length of time and take her out. Edith was very lonely, she had nobody belonging to her in the world and most of her old cronies had 'kicked the bucket' as she would say, a long time ago. She had no intention of kicking anything for as long as possible and always went around singing, 'Everybody wants to go to heaven, but nobody wants to die'.

'Of course Deirdre will have to see "Upstairs"' she said, 'but I'm sure that will be all right. After all Mabel recommended her.' 'Upstairs' was the tenant who had taken the whole top of the house twenty years ago when Edith had been left a widow and destitute, with nothing but this big house and not the vaguest idea of how to get tenants or how to earn a living. Mrs. Kelly — though Edith never called her anything but Kelly — had taken over the running of the house and invested some money in its upkeep, on the understanding that she would get the house when Edith died. So now Kelly would have to interview Deirdre to ensure that she was properly respectable and fit to live in 'her' house.

Kelly was always perfectly dressed, perfectly groomed, lipsticked and nail-varnished. With her blonde waved hair she looked like something out of the 1940's. She had a husband whom one hardly ever saw or heard and a slinky Persian cat of whom one heard and saw plenty. I had to hand it to her, she kept the house and the gardens in perfect order, she could be said to have discreet good taste. There were only two bells on the front door in case people on the road would realise there were tenants in the house. Edith and I shared one, the other was Kelly's. Respectability was the keynote of Kelly's existence. If she had found out that I was pregnant, not only would she have had me out of the house, but she'd blame Edith for having me there in the first place.

'Let's have a drink to cheer ourselves up,' I said to Edith. She produced a bottle of sherry and I had some brandy. We drank each other's health and toasted the new tenant and promised each other great times.

'Oh, by the way,' Edith said as she hobbled off to bed pleasantly jarred, 'Deirdre would like to move in in two weeks, if that is all right with you. Of course I don't want to rush you . . . '

'That's fine, Edith. No problem, I'll be out by Friday week.'

The next night we found a place in Phibsboro. We called on one of the houses on our list and the landlady said the flat was in another house several streets away. It had two rooms. A double flat, she kept calling it. The rent was £8 per week, and I wrote a cheque and told her I'd move in the following Friday. On the way home Joan and Susan were delighted, and I couldn't blame them. They had given up nearly all their evenings searching with me, and they had had enough.

I tried to feel some enthusiasm as I sat in my beautiful flat, realising that I would have to leave it in a week. But at least I had someplace to go, it seemed to be a fairly quiet district, the landlady wasn't living on the premises, it wasn't too bad really, with a bit of paint . . .

'It's the bloody black hole of Calcutta. It's a dive. It's got no water, no bathroom, the toilet is down through someone else's kitchen. The landlady was staring at you already, in a few months she'll have you twigged, you can't rear a child in that place.'

It was true the place was a dive. I had been so desperate to get someplace that I had tried to pretend it was all right. I felt completely hopeless, not angry or annoyed, just hopeless and dejected. I felt that I had failed and that I couldn't gather the energy to start searching for another place. I sat and stared at the door and the answer came to me. I didn't have to put up with this anymore. I could go out the door and down the road. Just a few hundred yards away was the canal. I could solve the whole problem by just walking into it. There seemed to be no point in struggling anymore, no place to go, nobody who could help. Would it be quick? The canal was very deep there . . . I was a very good swimmer . . . if I went in with all my clothes on I'd probably go down fairly fast . . . My eyes were riveted on the door, as if I was afraid that it might open of its own accord, terrified in case I was serious about drowning myself, yet fascinated by the thought of the dark deep water with the lights from the street lamps shining on it.

'So now we're into the realm of high drama, we're actually going to drown ourselves. Look, girleen, it's not a suitable night to be drowning yourself anyhow. Of course you can do it, but wait until you have a nice

summer's evening when it's warm and balmy, you don't want the added discomfort of icy cold water, now do you? Anyway, if you did drown yourself, you might end up in a worse pickle than you are in now. Look come on, snap out of it, there must be some other way.'

'What other way?' I paced the floor, smoking one cigarette after another. Christ, I wouldn't have to bother drowning myself, I'd die of nicotine poisoning anyway. I'd have to give up the fags. I went through the *Evening Press* again. Flats to Let. Apartments to Let. Houses for Sale. Houses to Let. Land for Sale. Caravans for Sale.

Caravans for Sale! Of course, why didn't I think of it before? Rolon were advertising mobile homes on easy hire purchase terms. I'd buy a mobile home. To hell with that dingy flat, no child of mine was going to be brought into a place like that. Tomorrow I'd buy a caravan.

XIII

When I told the girls the next morning they were in despair. They thought they had had me fixed at last, and now we were off on another wild-goose chase. It was hard to make them understand the desperate need I had for someplace where I could feel secure, someplace where I could make a home for my baby without the fear of being thrown out at any minute. I rang Rolon. Of course I could buy a mobile home. Did I have a site?

'A what?'

'A site, a place to park it.'

Oh Christ! I never thought of that. Never mind. We set off at lunch time to go to the Rolon headquarters in Santry. We couldn't move across the city; in an hour we had only gone a few hundred yards. Traffic was jammed in every direction. In the end we had to turn and get back to the office as best we could. That evening we discovered that a young garda had been shot dead in a bank raid on the quays, leaving a wife and young family, God help them. And I thought I had problems. That's why the traffic had been so bad, there were massive road blocks all over the city.

I rang Rolon again. They only sold new homes, they told me, and I'd have to find my own site. The best thing for me to do was to look for a secondhand place which already had a site. I searched the papers again. There were secondhand mobile homes for sale, and on Saturday morning Joan came with me to look at one. It was difficult to find. To get to it we had to veer off to the left on a very bad bend on the main road to the North. The site was much lower than the main road, and you'd pass it ten times without seeing it. We drove down on to the site. On either side there were caravans parked, each with its own little garden and a fence around it. The one we were looking for, number six, was down on the right hand side. The 'For Sale' sign was still up.

'Would you like to see around it?' asked Mr. Breen, the owner, when we told him we had come in reply to the advertisement. We nearly wet our knickers with excitement. The place was perfect, exactly what I needed. Inside the door was a little hallway, on the left was a sitting room and on the right a kitchen and behind that a good sized bedroom. Between the kitchen and sitting-room was a lovely little bathroom. All the essential furniture was in every room.

I tried to be casual as I asked the price. £400 cash and take over the Hire Purchase Payments at £16 per month. The £16 was all right, but he might as well have talked about £4,000 as £400, there was no place I could raise that kind of money. Only recently I had had a letter from my bank manager asking me what I intended to do about my overdraft. I could write back now and say 'double it'!

'I'm very interested,' I said, trying to keep my voice calm. 'I'll be back again this afternoon.'

'That's fine, I'll be here until six.' He looked as though he didn't really expect to see me again.

'You don't really think you can buy it, do you?' Joan said the minute we got into the car. 'Where on earth would you get that kind of money?'

'I haven't a clue, but I've got to have it. It's exactly what I need. It's got plenty of space, it's comfortable, no one would ever find me there. Oh Joan, I've got to have it. God, are you listening? Please God, make the money come from someplace, honestly, I need it!' I often roared at God when I really needed something very badly.

We drove back to my flat. But instead of going in, we

sat in the car outside the house, going over and over, around and around all the possible ways in which I could possibly hope to raise four hundred pounds. No matter how hard we tried, nothing seemed to work. Four hundred pounds was simply too much. . . . Suddenly I saw Eric! He had come out of his block of flats and was getting into his car, right in front of us. In a flash I lurched out of my car, ran over, and hammered on his window. He peered out at me and unlocked the passenger door. I got in and started talking fast.

'Eric, I've got to have four hundred pounds in a hurry, I've got to buy a mobile home, I know you've got plenty of money, you must let me have some!'

Considering that I had nearly deballed him a few nights ago, he was relatively civil. 'I haven't got that kind of money,' he muttered reluctantly. 'I'd have to get it, it would take time . . .'

'Damnation, it's not an awful lot of money,' I protested. 'Surely you could get it from the bank. I could get it myself, for God's sake, if I didn't already owe them so much. How come you were going to be able to get me money for an abortion?'

He didn't seem to be able to figure that one out.

If only I didn't owe the bank so much money; if only I hadn't always spent every halfpenny I earned as well as all I could borrow from them; if only I had some money saved — I wouldn't have to be here begging to try to get a roof over my child's head. I had to get the caravan. What would I do if I lost my job and had no money? I'd end up in a mother and baby home. The thought sent shivers through me.

'Eric, please,' I begged, 'I know you have money, you live in that expensive flat, you have no one else to spend it on. . . .' Suddenly, it became crystal clear to me that I was only wasting my time, the bastard had no intention of giving me anything. 'Oh, bugger off,' I yelled as I slammed out of his car and back to my own.

Joan was obviously waiting to hear what was going on but I didn't tell her. Instead we went over to Susan's house to see what she thought. She was up to her neck in a gluttony of baking when we called, but we dragged her away to see the caravan. Mr. Breen was surprised to see us again so soon, but he showed us around once more. 'Take it,' Susan said under her breath when she'd seen it all. There was a quiet certainty about Susan that never failed to amaze me. She knew I hadn't two coppers to rub together, but 'take it' she said as if she was talking about a lollipop.

'I'll take it,' I said to Mr. Breen, equally casually. Joan looked as if she didn't know whether to stay or go.

'Well, of course you will have to pay me a deposit,' Mr. Breen said.

'That's no problem,' I said, taking out my cheque book and writing a cheque for £200. 'Will that be all right? I'll want to move in next Friday night.'

'Oh, fine, but I'll need the other £200 before you move in, and we'll need to go to the hire purchase company to sign a new agreement.'

'I'll have the balance of the money next Friday night, and whenever it suits you, we can go to the hire purchase company.' I gave him my phone number at work, he gave me a receipt for £200. I shook hands with him. The three of us left. I was in a state of shock, the two girls were speechless.

'For God's sake let's go down and have a drink,' I suggested. We went into the nearest pub. I had a double brandy, Susan was a Pioneer and only drank orange, Joan had a gin.

'I thought I'd never keep a straight face when you wrote the cheque!' Susan laughed. 'But at least I have to hand it to you, you did it with a flourish. What on earth made you give him two hundred pounds? Fifty would have done for a deposit. That man thought all his birthdays were coming together.'

'Oh well, what's the difference? Fifty or two hundred, I've no money anyway, but I've got to get it pretty fast. That cheque will be through my bank by Wednesday at the latest and there will be hell to pay.'

'But the banks are on a go-slow,' Joan threw in. 'Maybe

your cheque won't get through that quickly.'

The banks had been on a go-slow for ages. There was even talk of them closing down — sweet Jesus, if only they would!

'Lord, Lord, are You listening?' I was saying my prayers out loud again. 'Just a little miracle, Lord, 'twould be no bother to You, just help the banks to close for a while — two months? a month? All those poor bank clerks really need a break, and You could easily do it if You wanted to.

'For heaven's sake will you shut your mouth,' Susan hissed, her face red with embarrassment, 'half the people in the bar are looking at you.' Sure enough some heads were turned, and no wonder, because there were the three of us sitting in a corner of the bar and me with me eyes turned up to the ceiling, haranguing the Lord, articulating loudly the not so secret wishes of most of them. Of course lots of people would love it if the banks closed. I could have led a pray-in there and then had I wanted to.

However God only helped those who helped themselves, I always believed, which still left me with the problem of where to get the four hundred pounds I needed. We agreed that the caravan was marvellous from every point of view. If only I could get the bloody money. I had one very strong hope, I had an aunt in England who had a bit of money. I felt sure she'd lend it to me. I'd pay her back at whatever rate of interest her money was earning. I felt nearly certain that she'd give it to me.

XIV

'You must admit you are being very selfish. I know it will be very hard for you, but you've got to have that baby adopted.'

I had asked Rob Gladstone to come and see me, and he came the following afternoon. We had got to know each other when I worked down the country. He was my counterpart in a company we dealt with in Dublin and over the years we had become firm friends. Since I came to Dublin we often met for drinks or lunch to discuss our various work problems or whatever.

I'd told him that I was pregnant and that I intended to keep the baby, and I knew that what he said was motivated by a genuine concern for me and the child, so I was determined to try to make him understand my reasons.

'Now listen to me, Rob,' I said to him, 'keep your mouth shut and listen and try to understand what I'm saying to you. I honestly believe that the best thing for me to do is to rear my child myself. I've got a pretty good job, as you know, and if I can stay in it and get back to work after the baby is born, I'll be able to afford to give it as good a life as most children have.'

'Ah, there you are already.' He couldn't shut up any longer. 'Even if you do succeed in staying in that job, who's going to mind the baby while you are at work?'

'There's bound to be a nursery someplace. I haven't quite figured it out, but there must be one. Lots of women go out to work now and someone must be looking after their babies.'

'Yes, but what kind of a way is that to rear a child? Letting somebody else do it for you? Sure the baby won't even know who its mother is.'

'Ah, for heaven's sake stop talking nonsense. How is it that for centuries the upper classes have always had someone to rear their children, in fact some of them hardly ever saw their kids at all. But has anyone ever suggested that that did the children any harm? Oh no, and why? because they are wealthy and rich and have lots of power. But now that the same facility is being extended to working people in the form of nurseries or crêches, there's an outcry. I'd much rather have my child minded with a lot of other kids in a nursery for a few hours a day, than hand it into the complete control of some nanny.'

'Yes, that's all very well, but what happens when the child goes to school?'

'Oh for Christ's sake, Rob, I don't know what happens when the child goes to school. It's not even born yet, and you're sending it to school. I can't think that far ahead. But I know that if I can manage for the first twelve months then I'll manage after that. And I'll tell you what else I don't know before you start asking. I don't know what I'll tell the child about its father, I don't know how I'll tell it I was never married. I don't know how I'll tell it the law calls it 'illegitimate'. There are a hundred things I don't know — but I'll tell you what I do know. I know that I can love my child better than anyone else. I know that when the questions come, I can answer them. It's only grown-ups who can't face facts, children can absorb any kind of information as long as there's no fuss and drama made out of it. I remember when I was a child, there were always mysteries and tight-lipped silences when you came into a room where grown-ups were talking. I remember I used to be terrified of all the dreadful things that were being kept hidden from me. What would adoptive parents do when my child started asking questions? How would they be able to tell it who it looked like? What auld great aunt had the same colour hair as it? Where it got such and such a strange mannerism from? Where its artistic qualities might come from, or if it's pure thick, sure there's bound to be some ancestor it took after! Nobody would even know if the child was going to marry its natural brother or sister. No, Rob, I'm the best one to answer my child's questions, not adoptive parents, however good they may be.'

'But the child will have no father . . . '

'Millions of children have no father, and divil a bit of harm it does them. It's not the fact the child will have no father that matters in this fucking country, but the fact that I have no marriage certificate. What a nation of hypocrites we are! We all know that every year thousands of women get married who are pregnant, but as long as they have big white weddings and the priest blesses them, that's fine. It's not the sex outside marriage that is taboo in this country, it's being found out. If I had an abortion or had my baby adopted that would be fine. But by keeping it it is going to be a living proof that I broke the eleventh commandment: "Thou shalt not be found out". Somehow or another I swear I'll rear my child free of the mockery of Christ that goes on in this country!' I had talked myself to a standstill.

'Now you listen to me,' he cut in. 'I believe you are right to keep your baby. I just wanted to make sure that you had thought about all the problems. Just one more thing, and I won't say another word. Do you realise that keeping the baby practically rules out any chance of marriage?'

'Yes, Rob, I've thought about that,' I laughed wryly, 'Irishmen all want sex before marriage, but they want to marry virgins. It's a bit of a conundrum. Never mind, you know marriage has never been on the top of my list of priorities. If I ever do think of marrying, it will be to a man who doesn't think that his prick is God's gift to women!'

'You never lost it,' he laughed. 'Now I've got something to tell you. Vera and I applied to adopt a baby last week.'

'Rob, I'm sorry.' I was completely stunned. 'I'm sorry for all the things I said, I didn't mean to hurt you, oh, why didn't you tell me!' I started sobbing. He had to take me by the shoulders and shake me to make me stop.

'Because I wanted you to say what you thought. You haven't hurt me, I believe in what I'm doing and I believe in what you are doing, all right?'

'Oh, Rob, you and Vera will be marvellous parents, it's just that I couldn't give away my baby, I must keep my baby.' I was still blubbering like a fool.

'Hmm, now who's being melodramatic? Pull yourself together, have a fag.' He stuck a cigarette in my mouth and lit it for me. 'I'm going to get you a cup of tea. I'll tell you what, we're hoping for a girl, you have a boy and we'll marry the two of them off.'

XV

It was now that I made my first big mistake. I rang my aunt in England and asked her for £300. I was bitterly disappointed when she refused, saying her money was all tied up in Ireland and she couldn't lay her hands on it. I just couldn't believe my bad luck.

My aunt Ethel was the younger of my mother's two sisters and had worked in England for years as a priest's housekeeper and had never married. Every year she came home for a month in the summer. Since I'd moved to Dublin I'd meet her at the airport, she'd stay with me for a week and then I'd drive her to wherever she was going. She had been the most stable element in my childhood. Always coming home in the summer, always fat and jolly, always bringing us presents. For every emergency aunt Ethel was sent for, and since all of the rest of my mother's family lived in one small town — actually in two small streets adjoining each other — there were lots of emergencies.

Auntie always came. Once or twice I remember her coming with her apron still on, having left her kitchen, thrown a coat on her shoulders and gone straight to the airport. My mother and several of her friends were married to men who drank a lot, gave them very little money, hit them an odd thump and managed to make everybody's life miserable most of the time. My aunt on the other hand had a good job, a lovely home, plenty of money for

elf and a very comfortable life which she obviously
oyed. Yet the other women bestowed a kind of knowing
ty on her because she hadn't got a man. I could never
make out why my aunt should want a husband like either
my father or his male neighbours . . .

I remembered that several years ago, she had said if any
of us ever wanted money to be sure and ask her for it.
Now I had taken her at her word.

And then I made my second bad mistake. Out of my
three sisters, I knew the one living in County Wexford
had some money to spare. I was not very close to her, and
would have been much happier writing to one of the
other two in West Cork and England. But I knew they
couldn't afford to help me. So I gritted my teeth and
wrote to Jane, asking her straight out for two hundred
pounds.

The minute I posted the letter I knew it was the most
stupid thing I could possibly have done. I had been determined to keep my family out of it, but now I had drawn
them all down on top of me like a wasp's nest. My parents
were dead and there were just three sisters and two brothers,
all married. I had figured that since I rarely saw any of
them I could easily stay out of the way until after the
baby was born. Then I could tell them and they could
like it or lump it. One thing I was sure of, my loyalty lay
with the child inside me, not with any grown-ups who
should be well able to look after themselves. I was also
completely certain that anyone who slighted my child
need never come near me. I kept hoping that perhaps she
would send me the money without asking any questions,
but I knew that I was only fooling myself. I had written
to her on Saturday night. By Tuesday I had worked
myself into such a state of tension that I could hardly eat
or sleep. On Wednesday morning the call came to the
office. Susan put it through, wishing me luck. I was
shaking as I pressed the button. Her voice was tight at
the other end of the phone.

'I got your letter, what do you want two hundred
pounds for?'

'I'm in a spot of bother,' I was trying to keep my voice casual, 'please just send the money, I'll pay it back fairly soon.'

'I can't just give you two hundred without knowing what it is for, what kind of trouble are you in?'

'It's the car,' I stammered, 'I need to have the car repaired and it will cost that much.'

'Stop telling silly lies!' I should have known she wouldn't buy that, she knew I'd never ask her for money just to get a car repaired. 'If you can't tell me what it is for, then I'm not giving you the money. I can't stand here all day.' She was putting down the phone.

'I'm pregnant,' I wailed, hoping in some desperate way that she might soften and maybe even give me some support.

'Oh my God! I knew it, I knew it. You trollop, sooner or later I knew you'd do it to me . . . ' there were desperate gurgles and gasps coming from the other end of the phone.

'What's wrong, what's wrong?', I had to stop myself shouting.

'I'm dying, I'm dying, I'm going to faint, my heart is going to stop!' Oh Christ, typical, I was pregnant and she was going to faint.

'Look, ' I said as calmly as I could, 'don't worry, forget it, I don't need the money, I'll manage, I'm sorry for upsetting you. Honestly I'll be all right, it's not as bad as you think.'

'I'll be up on Friday, I'll bring the money then.'

'No, no, oh Jesus no, there's no need, send the money if you like, but there's no need for you to come, the journey is too long, oh please don't come . . . ' She had put down the phone. I was furious with myself. Why had I asked her? Why hadn't I stolen the bloody money? I could surely steal four hundred if I was any good at all. She was intent now on her pound of flesh, I knew, and by God she'd make sure she got it.

For the next few nights I packed my things and got everything ready to move. On Friday I begged Susan and Joan to come home with me from work. Neither of them could understand why I was in such a state just because my sister was coming; as far as they were concerned, if they were in the same situation as me they would expect their families to be the first to help them.

How could I explain to them that my family was not like theirs, that there was no real closeness between us? Oh, there was lots of superficial family togetherness, but except for my younger brother I never really got on very well with any of the rest of them. Maybe that was because the others were a lot older than me and had always bullied me and patronised me and were always trying to have me speak only when spoken to. They had always been brilliant at school, always top of their classes, perfect members of the Children of Mary and Children of Angels. I, on the other hand, was always in trouble, from the first day I went to school, when having told the nun my name, she said: 'Ah, so we've got another brilliant O'Mahony, another feather in the school cap. Doreen and Eleanor and Jane's little sister, how marvellous! I taught your mother and your aunts and your sisters and I'm sure you'll be a very good girl, just like them.'

I was barely four then, so I can hardly have made a conscious decision to rebel, but all through my early school days I heard nothing from the nuns but how brilliant the O'Mahonys were, how proud I should be to be one of them, how good and holy and pious they were and then, as time went by, what a shame it was that I was such a dunce, what had my holy mother done to deserve me? what had they done to deserve me? I was always in trouble, always asking the wrong questions, always getting caught doing what every other child did but with the sense to do it behind the teacher's back. I nearly caused two nuns to have apoplexy one day by interrupting the priest who had come to give us a lecture on the evils of mixed bathing.

I told him I didn't see anything wrong with boys and girls swimming in the same part of the river. The nuns decided against swooning, as it was a long fall to a hard floor. They fixed me instead with their beady eyes, full of promised retribution. The priest left the room like a whirlwind.

My mother was sent for, for the umpteenth time, and God was called on again to explain why He had sent such a monster into a good convent school to be a thorn in the side of her teachers and a heartbreak and scald to her good mother and brothers and sisters. I passed from one class to another with a sigh of relief from the teacher I was leaving and a look of determination on the face of the nun who was taking me on.

In sixth grade I remember being startled one day by the nun refusing to punish me for one of my usual escapades on the grounds that at least I wasn't sneaky and whatever I did I did in front of everyone, not like some people she could mention. I couldn't believe it! At last I had found someone who stuck up for me. For her I became a model pupil. For years I had really believed that I needed the approval of my family, until it dawned on me that it didn't matter, our lives were completely separate, it was really my friends who were important to me. What I needed from my family was their support. Not their approval, I didn't want that, just their support. To know that my child would have a family other than me. My hopes were pretty slim.

We had had everything ready since six o'clock and sat waiting for Jane to arrive. Susan and Joan sat silent, I walked around smoking and drinking endless cups of coffee. Finally, sometime after seven o'clock, the door-bell rang. The three of us looked at each other, like convicts saying our last farewell to freedom. Susan went to the door. It wasn't just my sister, it was the husband as well. They came in, obviously immediately resenting the fact that the girls were there and looking like the chief mourners at a multiple funeral.

'You don't look very pregnant,' she said, as if it was something else I had done out of spite.

'No, I know,' I answered lamely. Even though I must be three and a half months gone, I was still as slim as ever and wore a tight fitting suit without a bit of bother. Apart from my breasts, which only I knew about, nobody would ever guess that I was pregnant.

'How about some tea?' I asked, and immediately Susan and I ran away out to the kitchen. In a few seconds Jane followed us, intent on getting me on her own. I decamped back into the other room, leaving Susan alone with her. I knew it was a lousy thing to do, but I couldn't help it.

After about ten minutes it became obvious that Susan must be getting a grilling so I went back to the kitchen. Susan immediately fled, leaving me cornered.

The silence was murderous. Neither of us knew how to break it. Finally I spoke:

'Look, it won't be so bad, if I can have the caravan, I can make a grand home for the two of us.' That seemed to work on her like a whiplash.

'What do you mean? What two of you?' Her eyes were staring.

'The baby and me of course, who do you think?'

'Oh my God, you're not going to keep that baby! Oh God you wouldn't do that to us! What will I do? What will people say? I knew you'd do it to us! You couldn't be like everybody else and go to England, oh no, you have to parade your shame, you rotten filthy whore!' She was in full spate and nothing would stop her until she had her say. There was always a desperate anger and hatred inside her ready to be poured out at any opportunity.

God knows I had given her plenty of opportunity.

'Who is the father?' she said, desperately drawing in her breath in a hopeless effort at control.

'I won't tell you.'

'You mean you can't tell me!' she shot back. 'You bitch, you've probably hopped in and out of bed with so many men you haven't a clue who is responsible.' She was goading me into a reply so that a full scale row could ensue and I was too contemptuous of her to give her the satisfaction she wanted. I stood with my back to her, desperately clinging to the teapot full of boiling water. I should have poured it over her. I should have pushed her and kicked her out the front door and told her never to come near me again. They would have been decent things to do. But I wanted her two hundred quid, so I stood there and never opened my mouth. One rule I had made for myself, never to use people badly for my own ends. Now I let her debase herself to a degree from which it would take her years to recover. I hated and despised her, but I loathed myself even more. I decided it was probably true that all hatred of other people was reflected self-hate.

There was no break in the silence or the tension as we packed the two cars and moved to the caravan. I said goodbye to Edith, promising to call during the week. The ache was inside my belly at the hurt I knew she was hiding. Still Deirdre was coming, it would be all right. Jane wrote the cheque for £200 and Mr. Breen left. The caravan was mine. With obvious relief Susan and Joan left. All I had to do was hang on until Sunday and I would have the place to myself. Several times during the week-end Jane tried to make me tell her who the father was. She even tried pleading with me, assuring me that it was for my own good that she should know. I wouldn't answer her. I warmed to her husband when he told me that if I'd just tell him who the fella was he'd go and make smithereens of him for leaving a girleen in such a state. I believed him. He was a decent simple man, powerfully strong from a life-time fighting a living from the land. I looked at his hands lying quietly on his lap. He'd tear Eric skin from bone before the other fellow had time to think what was happening to him. I'd have applauded if it applied to someone else, but somehow I couldn't hand Eric over to him.

My pride wouldn't let me admit that a man had loved me and left me, that I had been used as the nuns had always warned us we'd be used if we ever succumbed to the bestiality of man (except in holy wedlock), that I hadn't been smart enough to get my man to marry me, because after all wasn't that what we'd all been reared on? Smart women exchanged sex for wedding rings and houses and respectability. Only fools of women let men have them before they had married them. I had always considered sex for marriage the most base form of prostitution and despised the women who bartered their bodies in such a way, at the same time admiring the women who plied their trade openly, giving a bit of comfort and sex for a bit of cash, losing their reputations and often their health and gaining no recognition from society for the fact that it was often their work which allowed the other holy whores to live their frigid lives in comfort. I often thought that men who married women because it was the only way they could bed them got a very bad bargain. But then they didn't deserve any better, because it was they who set the rules by which women debased themselves.

None of my thinking did me any good. I had broken the rules and I was going to have to pay. Still, I appreciated my brother-in-law's gesture. He cared about me, I felt, unlike my sister, who only cared about the effect I'd have on the neighbours — whoever they were.

Finally on Sunday they left, after dire warnings that I was not to tell anyone else, least of all my brothers and other sister. That I was not to be seen, that I must not let anyone know my name because of the disgrace to the family. That she would write and tell my aunt that I needed the money for the car, so that she wouldn't be suspicious. That it was no use talking to me because I obviously cared about no one but myself. That it was well my parents were dead, because if they weren't they'd die of shame. That her own life was ruined and she'd never recover from the shock. She never mentioned that a baby was to be born, that being pregnant might be frightening, that I might be worried living in the caravan on my own. But they went, and that was all that mattered. Oh, the relief!

XVI

Miracles can happen . . . On the evening of the fifth of May, nineteen hundred and seventy, the banks closed and the staff just faded away. If only I had waited . . .

XVII

At last I began to feel a bit more secure. I settled into the caravan and felt as though I'd always lived there. It was a much greater distance to the office, but I still got there every morning just before nine. I still used the flat as my address and nobody suspected that I wasn't still living there.

Bit by bit I began to learn more about my neighbours on the site. The caravan below mine was an enormous forty foot affair which protruded ten feet out beyond mine, effectively cutting me off from the rest of the site below it. Down to that point there were five caravans on either side of the road. Most of them were like mine, thirty feet long, each with a little garden surrounded by a fence. In all of them there seemed to be young couples with one or two children, except directly across the road from me, where there was a most extraordinary couple.

They looked as though they were both in their late sixties, both very thin and small and weathered. Beside their caravan was another big one which was packed with old clothes of all descriptions. They were dealers, and set off every morning around six, in a big van which he drove. In the evenings they'd roll home, both pretty sozzled, and as like as not they'd set in to having the mother and father of a row. They didn't believe in mealy-mouthed polite arguments behind closed doors, but let rip in style, sometimes carrying the fight out on to the road, beating, belting, and throwing things at each other, locking each other out and abusing each other with a variety of colourful language which I only wish I could repeat.

Sometimes he'd disappear in the van, but he'd always be back in the morning. I was beginning to wake most mornings before six and I'd often see them going out. She always dressed up as if she was going to the society wedding of the year, always with a different hat perched precariously on her head, and tiny dainty wisps of shoes with three-inch heels on which she balanced like a fairy. The lipstick and powder were in place and the earrings dangling. She had a fag hanging out of her mouth with an inch of ash on it that never seemed to fall off. One morning I woke in a panic realising that I was the object of her venom. I rushed out to the door and she was standing in the middle of the road in all her glory, fag in mouth, calling on God and all the Saints in heaven to give her the power to describe the kind of hungry bitch who would leave her car in the way of honest decent people, preventing them from turning their van and getting on with their day's work. I moved the car, trying several times to tell her that I hadn't really parked it deliberately in their way, but it was no use. She was still hurling abuse as they drove off. That evening she knocked at the door asking me not to take too much notice of her, she sometimes had a drop too much and it ran away with her tongue. A few mornings later she repeated the whole exercise.

Whenever the rows happened, you could see the curtains moving all up and down the site, and you knew that people were standing at their windows in terrified enjoyment. Nobody else on the site would have the guts to carry on like those two, being too respectable, and yet if respect was something one earned from one's fellow man, they were the most respectable pair around as far as I was concerned. If they had that much energy at that time of their lives, what must they have been like when they were young? And what were they like in bed? The mind boggled.

I discovered that directly behind the caravans opposite

mine was a drop of about ten feet into the filthy water of the river. It was a nightmare for all the people with young children on the site. The road, which was only hard packed sand and gravel, turned into a quagmire after a shower of rain. The water supply came from an open tank at the end of the site and was undrinkable, a fact which my doctor confirmed after he had analysed a sample. He told me not to drink it under any circumstances so I bought a five gallon drum and dragged it in and out of the car, filling it wherever I happened to be when it was empty. About half a mile up on the main road there was a pump, and sometimes I filled it there, but only when it was dark, because I was absolutely terrified of being seen by anyone I knew.

The landlord came around every week for the ground rent — thirty bob a caravan. The reluctance with which I told him my second name must have made him wonder about me, but he never made any comment. He was a big rangy man with a shock of red hair, all bulging muscle and very attractive if you like that sort of thing. He was an easygoing character and didn't fuss if you didn't have the rent exactly on time.

There were about sixty caravans altogether, mostly down below mine. For the majority of the couples, it was the first step to buying their own house, but of course Local Government didn't approve it, so it got no proper water supply. Typical of Local Government — they couldn't house the people themselves but frowned on any efforts at self-help. The place was riddled with gastro-enteritis and the women in particular lived in a constant state of fear and worry and anxiety. But there was nothing that anyone could do. If there were any complaints to the council they simply threatened to clear the site immediately.

None of this bothered me very much. I was safe. The banks were closed. Everyone said it would be a long strike.

If only I had waited another week, I need never have involved my sister and could have saved myself from all the drama and abuse. It would have been good never to have known what her reaction would be, not to have told her until after the baby was born, when perhaps she could have accepted it more easily. . . .

XVIII

On a Sunday afternoon early in May I was walking down Killiney hill, one of my favourite places when I wanted to be alone. The weather was still quite cold and I was walking all hunched up against the wind when I felt it. At first it was a faint fluttering and I wasn't quite sure, but then it came again very definitely, like butterflies' wings beating against my tummy. It was my baby moving. I stopped in my tracks, my face alight at the wonder of it. And then I remembered . . . I wasn't supposed to be pregnant, I was a disgrace and I had no right to be joyful about it. My face fell back into its habitual expression of frozen anxiety. It was months since I had smiled or really laughed, I realised. I looked around me furtively, there was nobody about. The baby kicked again, even stronger this time. To hell with people, I thought, only God could make this miracle of movement happen inside me, it was criminal to deny happiness.

I skipped down the hill, I hopped and jumped and twirled around, I climbed onto the wall separating the road from the cliff edge and yelled at the top of my lungs out across the bay. The seagulls that had been wheeling gently in front of me went screeching away in terror. I laughed out loud and settled myself down with my back to the wall facing out across the bay. I felt full of contentment and powerful knowledge, as if I held the secret of life going back beyond the bounds of time. Nobody could take this away from me, nobody could deprive me of the knowledge I held inside me. Why, oh why had the world become so complicated, that the circumstances of conception became more important than the fact that the miracle had happened, as if life could somehow be confined within the boundaries laid down by man?

Why had we women allowed ourselves to become so degraded, that we believed the fight for contraception and abortion was our way to liberation, denying our most powerful weapon of all — the ability to conceive and carry a child? How had we been sidetracked in our search for freedom into believing that our way lay in having the sexual freedom apparently enjoyed by men, which was after all only the freedom to be irresponsible? Had we been conned by men into believing they were free? How was it possible they had led us to believe that freedom was to be equal to them? What had men in their barren bodies once they had shot their seed? And no matter how many times they did it, what did it matter? The life must still develop in the womb of the woman and grow there and come out of her. Time and again, history had proved that there was nothing men could do that, given the same conditions, women couldn't equal. And yet the one thing we could do, the one extraordinary and mind-boggling ability which we have, was being downgraded and made little of.

A new understanding of, and admiration for women flooded through me, a new empathy with my mother whose life I had never considered very much. So she had felt this surging life inside her? It seemed as if I suddenly knew about my mother, understood that her life was not just a resigned drudgery, that she had felt inside her the secret power that is shared by women from one end of the earth to the other. I felt a desperate regret that my mother wasn't alive so that I could tell her that I knew, that I understood a little bit more, that I felt I was taking my place in the chain of life. 'Too Late the Learning,' but as I sat there looking out across the bay, I felt that somehow she knew and was glad for me.

An overwhelming pity for men flooded me. How could

they know or understand what women were about? How could they take a pregnancy seriously when it had such little personal significance for them? Somehow it was up to women to make them understand. I wanted Eric, physically and mentally and emotionally I wanted him then. He was the father of my child. I wanted him to care about the child, I wanted him to feel the joy I was feeling; somehow if I could get to him I knew I could convince him of everything, that there would be no more misunderstandings. I drove into town. As I got near the flat my conviction began to waver a little. If his car wasn't there I wouldn't stop, I promised myself. It was. The door was open. I climbed up the stairs and into his flat and into his arms and into his bed. We hardly said a word . . .

For several weeks things were beautiful. The office was calm, the caravan was great, I felt marvellous. Then, one morning, it seemed without any warning, I couldn't get into my clothes. Standing sideways in front of the mirror it seemed to me that my belly was enormous and that everyone must surely know I was pregnant. I was back to square one, there was no way I was going to survive. Even if I could afford new clothes, I felt it was essential to wear the same gear to the office for as long as possible — any change would only draw attention to me. When I had sat nursing my depression for the required amount of time, it finally occurred to me that I could get my trousers tied by using an enormous pin. That got me to work for that day, and at lunchtime I bought lots of elastic and hooks and eyes. That evening I doctored my trousers, sewing elastic on to the waist band, so that no matter how big I got, I could expand it. There was an enormous hole where my zip wouldn't close and my belly stuck out but that didn't matter, it was covered by my jumper. I developed an exercise for survival. Coming and going to and from the office I always draped a huge old báinín cardigan over my shoulders, on my arm I always carried a basket, nobody could really see your belly when you had a basket held in front of you. My legs swelled until they were the same size all the way down — which reminded me of the proverb:

'Irishwomen have a dispensation from the pope to wear the thick ends of their legs downward.' I never considered the proverb funny; and my legs weren't. They weren't painful, just uncomfortable and ugly to look at, and I couldn't get a shoe to fit me. My doctor told me there was nothing wrong and that I had better just get some suitable footwear, which seemed impossible until I found a pair of Scholls Exercise Sandals which I had discarded after wearing once.

They were perfect. The wooden soles gave me support and I was able to extend the straps as necessary. The weather was beginning to get warm at last, but I never discarded the báinín. Luckily I had the reputation of being the biggest perisher in the seven parishes, so apart from Susan's parents, who made a few comments about me roasting to death, nobody paid any attention to me.

And then I was jerked into another state of anxiety. My boss came down one day to discuss alternative arrangements for money, since it appeared that the bank strike was going to continue indefinitely, a state of affairs for which I was privately very grateful. We had decided on our arrangements, but he continued to sit there in the best of humour chatting casually about all kinds of things. He must have been talking for half a minute about how much he wanted to help unmarried mothers, before my mind registered what he was saying. He was the kind of person who never looked at you when he was speaking to you, so he never saw my face. He told me that he felt it was about time that he did something to help other people and that since he had an empty house in the middle of town, he would like to give it to unmarried mothers, either while they were pregnant or with their children. Several of them could live there for nothing, he said, and if I knew any, would I ever tell them and make the necessary arrangements?

I was back in the nightmare. I heard my voice calmly discussing the project with him, telling him what a wonderful idea it was and how kind of him to think of such a thing, that I didn't know anyone who would fit the bill at the moment, but if I did, I'd let him know. My mind was swirling. Did he know then? Was this his way of telling me that he knew I was pregnant and that he was offering me help? What else could it mean? It was just too much to be a coincidence. The perspiration was running down my back, the baby was kicking so that I was sure he could see the front of my dress bobbing up and down. What was I supposed to say? That yes, I was pregnant and that I badly needed help from anyone who would give it to me? Suddenly the thought of how easy it would make my life if my boss knew and supported me and assured me that my job was not in jeopardy, nearly made me blurt out the whole story. Instinct made me shut my mouth.

At lunch time Susan and Joan and I discussed it from every possible angle. We each arrived at the same conclusion — he didn't know, if he did he would be reacting completely differently, it was pure fluke that made him pick me, of all the people in the office to discuss his charitable enterprise for unmarried mothers with. But what really puzzled me was what had put unmarried mothers into his head in the first place? It wasn't as if they were people one heard about every day, I was desperately trying to find one and he was talking as if they were a dime a dozen.

That afternoon brought more disaster. Susan came down with the news. Richard was leaving. I was delighted. Though I genuinely liked the guy a lot, self-preservation was now my primary objective and having him out of the way would be a great relief. Though he had been as thick as thieves with the boss up to the night before, as far as we all knew, he had apparently had some frightful row with him to-day and was leaving immediately. I couldn't help it, I was thrilled. And then Susan produced the bad news. The whole place was closing down for three weeks from the 12th of July; everyone had to take their annual leave at the same time. I was desolate. That put an end to my plans. I had been determined to try and stay at work until the end of July or early August and with sick leave and holidays I'd have been fine. Having to take holidays in mid-July added three or four more weeks on to the time I'd have to be away from the office. The two girls tried to console me by telling me that I couldn't have stayed in the office that long anyway and that it didn't make any difference. I didn't agree with them. I was nearly six months pregnant and I was certain I was not noticeable. I still had the plan of the stuffed bra and extra roll-on to put into action.

XIX

About this time Joan's sister Aileen came home from Hong Kong. She was married to the first mate of a deep-sea vessel and she often came home for long stretches at a time. One Sunday afternoon I stupidly offered to drive her over to the National Maternity Hospital in Holles Street, where she had booked herself in for a check-up, because she was two years married and wasn't yet pregnant. Stupidly, because I didn't realise what I was letting myself in for. The place was like a railway station. People coming and going in all directions, one of the reasons being that it was visiting time on a Sunday afternoon. We couldn't have picked a worse time. As we stood waiting for her to check in there seemed to be nothing but enormously pregnant women everywhere, all with husbands in tow. One ward we could just see into was full of women waiting to go into labour, or in the early stages. There were loads of friends or relations around all the beds. My belly started doing somersaults. So this is where I would have to come on my own, with no husband and no relatives. I couldn't do it. Whatever happened I wasn't coming into a place like this, I'd die first, I'd have my baby at home, my doctor would have to do something about it. I looked at Aileen and the irony of the situation nearly made me scream. She was in a misery because she was married and wasn't pregnant, and I was in a misery because I wasn't and was. How was it, I wondered, that people who really wanted a baby couldn't have one, and people like me ended up pregnant without any bother? There was no figuring it out. I finally left Aileen in her little room and ran out of the place as fast as I could.

The next day I went straight down to my doctor at two o'clock, practically hysterical, telling him what had happened and that he would have to find someplace else for me to have my baby. He calmed me down, assuring me that I didn't have to go into Holles Street, that he would get me into a private nursing home, that he would make all the arrangements, that I had nothing to worry about except paying for it.

As usual when I was with him, my problems and worries nearly seemed to dissolve. He had so much strength in him that he poured it into me without any bother. He joked about how pretty I was looking and said it was obvious that I needed to be pregnant. He assured me that I was going to have the most beautiful baby boy that he had ever delivered in his long career. He knew it was a boy, he said, by the shape of it. Considering that he hardly ever looked at me, let alone examined me, I wondered how he knew that, but there it was. If he said I was going to have a beautiful baby boy, then that is what I'd have.

He asked me again about the child's father. I evaded the question. How could I tell him about how I was carrying on with Eric? And carrying on was the only word for it. I was making all the running. Several times a week I called into the flat and screwed him with an energy that left him exhausted. Often, on my way to collect money for the office in the morning, if he was there I did the same thing. I had myself convinced that for the sake of my child, the father must love me now. Sometimes I worried in case it was dangerous to be making love when I was so pregnant, but most of the time I stayed on top, riding him with fury, pushing him into me as if I could make him touch the child inside me. Often in the mornings I literally left a thousand pounds lying on the floor while I goaded him into wanting me. If he tried to resist I knew how to get at him until he took me with a despair that made me triumphant.

I convinced myself it was love, it was for my child. I refused to admit that I was a predator and blocked the word rape out of my mind. In my heart I knew that Eric didn't want me, that he was getting more and more confused as I was getting more and more adamant that we were having a beautiful love afair. I was so sexy that I just had to have him, but how could I say that? Sometimes when I arrived back at the office with a load of cash, I carried on an imaginary conversation with my boss.

He: Miss O'Mahony, where on earth have you been? Surely it didn't take you all this time to collect that money?

Me: Well, it's like this, Sir. You see, I had to fuck the father of my child and it took longer than usual to seduce him.

He: I beg your pardon.

I had gone completely daft and didn't even know it. How could I tell all this to my darling doctor? I couldn't bear to lose his respect, so I kept my eyes on the ground and told him that I had lost track of Eric. He went into one of his long spiels about how badly done by women were. Sometimes he annoyed me when he went into one of these rhapsodies. He idolised women and could go on for ages about how great we were and what we had to put up with, and how there wasn't a man in the world who could hold a candle to us. Which was all very fine. I had lots of women friends, I liked women, but they could be an awful drag. I really preferred the company of men, though I had to admit that I'd be lost without the support of Susan and Joan now. Still, there was no need to overdo it.

I told him about the holiday arrangements in the office and that it seemed as though I would have to have sick certs for ages, and how would he possibly manage to give them to me. He told me to shut up and mind my own business, and leave all that to him, that he would be able to give me any certs that I needed, and for as long as I needed them, that there would be no problem and that if 'that fellow down there' as he referred to my boss, dared to upset me, I was to let him know and he would sort him out. I believed every word of it.

XX

I got a letter from my friend Joseph which really made me laugh.

At the moment June 9th and His Lordship and St. Brendan's Cathedral is most on me mind. It's hard to revise all the last few years' study when you know you are nearly baked and ready for consumption. Me mother is fluttering around at home making 'arrangements' and all. Oh God, this study would break your heart. There has been so much change and confusion in recent years that the thought of putting all we have learnt into a coherent frame is mind-boggling!

In the summer I was thinking of getting the loan of a Honda and moving around the country — say up North and maybe Kerry — storing up memories to take abroad with me, though I have some pretty potent ones already. If you want to come tell me.

Au revoir, sweet bitch.

Say a prayer for us,
love,
Joseph.

The 'if you want to come' was what made me laugh. It was so ambiguous that it could easily have referred to going around Ireland on the back of a Honda. Apart from the fact that Joseph couldn't drive anyway, the picture this conjured up really tickled me. A newly ordained priest and an unmarried pregnant woman? Of course I knew that he was asking me to come to his ordination, and the fact that I would have to refuse made me very sad. We had been friends for so long, and on the biggest day of his life I wouldn't be there to rejoice with him, but I couldn't risk it. Even though Joseph knew I was pregnant and was quite prepared to have me there, I'd be so uneasy in meself I'd probably just ruin the day for the two of us. The thought of him being ordained filled me with fear, why I couldn't really say, but he seemed so young. He had gone straight from school into a seminary, so how in God's name could he know what he was doing? I had begged him to take two or three years off and go away and work somewhere before he took the final plunge. He was equally adamant that he knew exactly what he was doing. It was typical of the Catholic Church, I thought, with pure undiluted prejudice, that they would take kids of fourteen or fifteen and hang on to them for six or seven years and then make them take vows which were supposed to last a lifetime.

So we didn't go around Ireland on a motor bike, and I didn't attend the ordination. To make up for this lack of involvement, Joseph decided that I must have a special mass all to myself, and so his second mass was arranged in the private chapel in a convent in the centre of Dublin. We were invited about a week in advance, Susan and me. A friend of Joseph's who had been in the seminary with him, but had had the sense to leave before being ordained, would serve the mass.

I wanted to be there, but the terror of whether or not these nuns would know I was pregnant kept rearing its head. Susan kept telling me that whether they knew or not didn't matter a damn, but it was no good. I was gone completely neurotic about secrecy and people knowing my name, and glared balefully at any friend who used my surname in introducing me to anyone. I was now totally convinced that I was bringing shame and disgrace on my family name — for the first time in a thousand years.

The insanity of this mental state led to a further comic-opera scene a few days later in town. For weeks we had been talking about the need for me to buy a maternity roll-on. I was six months gone and it would be a further help in keeping me in shape. However, to carry out this daring deed needed terrific forward preparation, it seemed to me. I'd have to have a wedding ring and I'd have to be properly composed to carry off the scene. After all there were only a million people wandering around Dublin, and obviously they were watching me.

One day in Henry Street, shortly before the proposed mass, Susan suddenly said, 'Hey, let's go and get that roll-on now, you could do with it for Saturday.' Without waiting for all my arguments about why it couldn't be done, wedding rings, proper preparation, etc. she shot into Arnotts with me on her heels. Down to the end of the shop we went, and lo and behold a whole section was given over to maternity wear. There was no one around and happily we examined all the corsets, bras, swim-suits, slips, and nighties, all designed to enhance and show off to the best advantage the beautiful bump. Without any indication that she had ever been any place else, a lady assistant suddenly appeared in front of us. Clad entirely in black, her enormous bosoms moulded into smouldering sedation, steel rimmed spectacles hanging by a black beady chain around her neck and her steel grey hair piled high on her head in a formidable bun, she was straight out of a book.

'Can I help you, ladies?' she asked in a most ordinary voice. I wanted to run, but my feet riveted themselves to the floor, so I just stood speechless, my face glowing red like a beacon. Susan, seeing that I was going to do nothing, and obviously fed up at the idea of another abortive trip, stuttered,

'Well, ah, yes, you see, I am, well, thing is this, you see, I need am, well it's for my cousin, you see, she lives down the country.'

With not the flicker of an eyelid, or any indication that she sensed agitation in either of us, the saleslady said,

'I see, what is it then that you want for your cousin?'

We stared at each other. My face was burning, Susan's was chalk white. The assistant looked as if this kind of thing was an everyday occurrence. Then in a perfectly normal voice Susan said,

'We want a maternity roll-on, please.' I held my breath and looked carefully around from the corners of my eyes. It had been said, the roof hadn't fallen in, Arnotts was still standing. I was just gulping in a breath of pure relief when the assistant said,

'Have you any idea what size your cousin might want? What height is she? How pregnant is she?' Susan turned towards me, examined me minutely, turned back to the assistant and without a glimmer of a smile said,

'She is medium height and about six months pregnant.' The woman showed us a variety of garments and finally after a lot of discussion as to which one would best suit Susan's cousin, the lady parcelled it up and handed it to Susan.

'Have you the money?' says she to me, handing me the parcel. I fumbled in my bag and produced the three pounds and some shillings required, and finally we left the shop.

'You know you are quite mad,' Susan said in a matter of fact voice as we hurried up Henry Street. What could I do but say yes.

The mass was scheduled for seven o'clock, and we had been told to be there about fifteen minutes before, to meet the nuns. We drew up outside the convent and for the hundredth time I said to Susan, 'Am I noticeable, do you think?' For the hundredth time, with total patience and supportive lies, she said,

'Of course not, no one would ever guess.'

The door was opened by a young nun who led us to the parlour and told us that we would be going into the chapel in a few minutes, Father was just robing. Father! God! She was talking about Joseph, he was now solemnly being called 'Father' and taking on himself the awesome

115

and terrible responsibility of turning bread and wine into 'the body and blood of Christ.' My mind flipped, I couldn't remember what I was doing there . . . I must get out for Christ's sake . . . I had never believed in transubstantiation — but we were already in the little chapel. Polished wood, sanctuary lamp lighting, smell of incense, evening light streaming through the stained glass window behind the tiny altar — peace, serenity, faith.

There were only nine kneelers, spread apart in rows of three. Susan took the centre one in the first row, I went straight in behind her and the nuns filled in the others. There was a small prayer bench attached to the kneeler, with a space for prayer books, and against which one could lean, but there was no place to sit. I started to panic again, would I be able to stick it out? Would I faint? What would Joseph's friends think? The tension was knotting inside in my belly — my back was aching — the roll-on was cutting the insides of my legs — my knickers and tights seemed to be stuck up my arse. Fuck Joseph I thought, why the hell did he get me into this? All those prissy nuns beside and behind me, were they all staring at me? Did they know?

The incongruity of the clothes I had on me suddenly hit me, and I farted in an effort not to laugh out loud. What on earth had possessed me? I had on a white fitted crocheted dress, a blue crocheted poncho, and a white mantilla on my head — the colours of the Immaculate Conception. Was I trying to make a case for myself? Anyone would think I was trying to make a sick joke, but I hadn't even thought about what I was putting on, except in so far as it made me less pregnant looking. Oh well, Mary was supposed to have felt alone, when she was carrying Jesus, but that was for a different reason, it was because she couldn't be telling people that the child she was carrying was the Son of God. When did men realise that if a woman could be the Mother of God, then women could get all kinds of ideas into their heads — they might want to become priests, bishops — a woman might even want to become pope. That would never do.

It was a stroke of genius on the part of the Church to turn Mary into a Virgin Mother, ensuring that the fact of a woman being the Mother of God in no way gave women any sense of power, and effectively removing her forever from the company of her sisters, for who could be like her? Creating a Virgin Mother who could only produce her God-Man at the behest of men — overshadowed by the Holy Ghost, negating our power of motherhood and making it worthless, because in becoming mothers we weren't virgins, twisting and distorting until they had us so screwed up that we believed our bodies were unclean after giving birth, so that we had to be churched. Received back into the fold by a man. Prayed over, candled over and told we were now fit to receive their sacraments again. And we swallowed it all, we grovelled and apologised and eagerly accepted their forgiveness for the uncleanliness of our motherhood. The injustice and manipulation of it made me want to scream. Why did we put up with it? Why didn't women in the Catholic Church now rise up in their wrath and put an end to it? Why not restore Mary to her rightful place as the all-powerful person who could produce her God-child without any help from men — father, son, or holy ghost? How was it that billions of women could be conned into believing that a just almighty being had created them second class citizens? All the power of the Roman Church was held by men in the name of a male God.

Joseph swept out on the altar, followed by his friend. The beautiful mass robes were new and fitted him perfectly. So it was true, he was a priest — 'a priest forever according to the order of Melchisedech.' I wanted to moan out loud in a welter of regret and nostalgia and remembering. Remembering the evenings in Howth, snuggled in the heather, nearly making love but never doing it. The evenings that the two of us had taken Edith out to shows and pubs and hotels, she always a bit puzzled by Joseph's clerical clothes and never quite sure how to address him. Had we been in love? Yes in a way, but not the kind that would have stood up to any reality . . .

117

'Let us pray for the unmarried mother in our community . . .' Yee-eeks! My eyes focused on Joseph's face; he was standing facing us with his hands stretched out, praying for me. Did everyone know he was praying for me? Nothing disturbed the serenity of the tiny chapel. I tried to drag myself together and forced my mind back to what was going on. It was coming up to the consecration. The altar was in the Vatican II style with the priest facing out to the congregation. Pope John had a lot to answer for, I mused, doing away with the Latin mass and making the priest face the people while he was saying the new mass. At least when they had their backs turned to us we didn't have to watch the spectacle of them stuffing flesh and blood down their throats. Another contradiction of the Catholic Church — they condemned cannibalism, yet the central and most important part of their religion was transubstantiation — the turning of the bread and wine into the body and blood of Christ — no second class symbolism for them, oh no, bread and wine must be turned into flesh and blood and eaten — ugh!

Why had I come? It seemed as though I was making a mockery of everything these people held sacred, yet that wasn't true. Joseph had wanted us to share this, it meant a lot to him. Now the strain was too great, but in memory we would share something good. The consecration was over for me, Susan was receiving Holy Communion, we were all supposed to give each other the kiss of peace — Pope John again. Joseph gave us a little homily on the need for true charity towards each other. At last it was over. 'Go in peace' and the blessed, heartfelt 'Thanks be to God.'

XXI

Joan got herself a new job and I didn't see her for several weeks. I missed her, but knew she was far better off to have changed. One day she rang me to say she must see me urgently at five. She sounded very mysterious, but wouldn't enlighten me, so I had to content myself with waiting. I hated waiting. I could ring her up and ask her what it was about, make her tell me on the phone. It could hardly be anything very serious. Maybe her mother had found out I was pregnant. Hell, she could have told me on the phone. However, I'd know soon enough.

I sat in my little office, dreaming as I seemed to spend half of my time those days. The trees were in full leaf outside my windows, and surrounded me in a shady green world. The words from some poem straggled through my mind . . . 'Strode among the tree tops and was taller than the trees.' — what poem? I couldn't remember — yes I could, it was 'Lepanto', but I couldn't remember who wrote it — my memory was hopeless. My office was like a tree-house at this time of the year: The weather was boiling but the trees waved gently outside and at least made a semblance of coolness. I was in no humour for working — the heat was really getting me. I got up and paced the office. My legs were so swollen they were hideous, my ankles practically flopped down over the exercise sandals, which luckily I was still able to wear.

I wondered if Eric had got the letter yet from the solicitor and what his reaction would be. He was supposed to go into the solicitor's office that day and I wondered if he would. It was strange the way this situation had come about. I had become so neurotic about my name and people knowing who I was, that I was driving the few friends who were supporting me quite daft. Finally I had hit on the idea of changing my name by deed poll. If I was bringing such disgrace on my family, I decided, then I'd abandon it, I'd find a new name and they could all go to hell. Betty gave me the name of her solicitor, who she assured me was very kind and would help me without any bother.

I had made an appointment to see him and had sat in my usual terror in his office a week earlier. Finally I had been shown into his room and sat with a dry mouth waiting — for what?

'So, Mrs. O'Mahony, what can I do for you?' he asked in a mild voice.

'Well actually I'm not "Mrs",' I blurted. 'I wish to God I was, then I wouldn't be in this pickle — I wouldn't have the problems I have now.'

'Don't you believe it,' he said. 'Most of the people coming in here are married. Now, what's the big problem?'

Before I realised what I was doing, I had told him the whole story, about being pregnant, and not being married, and shaming my family, and having decided to change my name by deed poll. He listened without comment and yet extended such a feeling of sympathy and caring that I was nearly beginning to cry. He was probably in his fifties and looked as if nothing could penetrate the air of serenity that surrounded him. Reliability was the word that described him. Somehow one knew that he was a very reliable man. 'You see, that's the best thing', I stammered, coming to the end of my story, 'I'll be someone else, my child will have a different name. The only problem is I haven't got a lot of money just now . . .'

'Never mind the money,' he cut in, 'we'll sort that out another time. What you are deciding to do is a serious business. Why should you change your name if the one you have suits you? What name did you have in mind anyway?'

I didn't know. I had spent days trying to figure out what name I'd like, but none seemed to suit me — I could change to Eric's name, I supposed, but his name was horrid, I couldn't bear it.

'Oh, I don't know,' I sighed, 'any name will do.'

'Take my advice, leave your name alone and stop trying to complicate your life. Now, tell me about the father of this child — or did you manage it all on your own?'

The effort at a joke brought a vague smile to my face, and I told him all about Eric and buying the caravan and asking for money, which Eric wouldn't give me.

'Don't you think it would be more in our line to write that lad a letter? We'll tell him to get himself in here and sort this business out. He'll have to give you some money and take responsibility for this child. Now, give me his name and address.' For the first time since I got pregnant, I stuttered out Eric's full name and address.

'Let's hope that he pays up, and you won't have to take him into court.'

'Why, what would be bad about going into court?' I asked.

'My dear, I could not let you go through that humiliation, it is a dreadful procedure, you have to tell them every single fact about your relationship — no, I feel sure we will be able to get some money out of him without resorting to that. He is not married, is he?'

'Of course he's not married, what put an idea like that into your head?' It annoyed me the way people assumed one could know a guy as long as I knew Eric without knowing whether or not he was married.

'Now,' said Mr. Burke, 'there is no need to get up on your high horse, it's just that a lot of these jokers are.'

The feeling of being on the outside of some big conspiracy hit me again. How was it that my doctor and this solicitor spoke as if married men making women other than their wives pregnant was an everyday occurrence, and as if I was the only fool who didn't understand what was going on all around me.

'If it is necessary, we will go into court,' I said, and again Mr. Burke looked at me as if I had a hole in my head. 'There's no use writing threatening letters if we do not follow them through. Eric is the father of my child, he has some responsibility. I don't want a lot of money from him, just enough to tide me over, he has got plenty, I wouldn't ask him if I thought he couldn't afford it, and anyway he should legally acknowledge his own child.'

Mr. Burke sighed at me again. 'Very well, but I assure you if you go into that courtroom you will be torn asunder, and for what? The most you can get is one pound a week maintenance. It simply isn't worth it.'

I was too impatient to wait until five, so I left work at a quarter to and drove down to where Joan was working. At about five after the hour she appeared, took her time getting into the car and refused point blank to tell me anything until we had moved out of the rush hour traffic and were on our way to her house. There was no hurrying her, and I knew it, but I was getting more and more short-tempered. What on earth was the big secret? She insisted that we stop a few hundred yards away from her house, and settled herself down, enjoying the suspense and knowing that I was ready to explode.

'Now listen,' she finally said, 'for the past few days there has been a guy around here looking for you, he has been waiting outside our door every day, and last evening he called me and asked me to get you to meet him here to-day at 5.30.' She stopped breathless, looking at me for enlightenment.

'But who could he be? Why would anyone come looking for me in such a strange fashion? Honestly Joan, I don't know who it could be . . . '

She was looking at me in disbelief.

'Honestly,' I assured her, 'I haven't a clue, what is he like? Didn't you recognise him?'

She didn't. We went through all the possibilities, but nothing worked. Who could be trying to contact me and for what?

'Oh well,' Joan said philosophically, 'you'll just have to wait another ten minutes, he said five thirty.'

'Shit — it is all right for you to say that so calmly, but who the bloody hell could he be? I just can't make it out.' I had practically given up smoking, but I decided I needed one now; patience was never one of my virtues, and ten minutes seemed like eternity. At last a big green car pulled in just in front of mine.

'There he is,' Joan said excitedly, 'Do you know him?'

'Of course I know him, you amadán, that's Eric's friend Bill, you've met him several times.'

Joan swore she had never met the man, who was by now standing by my door, asking me to join him in his car. What on earth was going on?

'If I'm not back by tomorrow,' I muttered wryly, 'send for the cops.'

We sat in Bill's car. Not having a notion of what he wanted me for I waited for him to begin and he did. In a most conversational tone, he said, 'Eric's wife is in town. You should ring her and tell her you are pregnant.'

The silence went on and on. I wasn't there . . . I wasn't hearing . . . I wasn't speaking . . . I wasn't pregnant. My life wasn't in bits. I was somewhere, away, away. I wasn't having a child by a man who was already married and whose wife was now with him. The silence continued, I didn't breathe, if I breathed I knew the badness would come back and I'd be pregnant and not married and the father of my child would be married to another woman and I'd be s-c-r-e-a-m-i-n-g.

'Jesus, stop it,' he put his hand over my mouth and was holding me with his other arm around my shoulder. 'Whist now, sh-sh-h-h' he was saying. 'There now, take it easy, I thought you knew, surely you knew Eric was married?'

Of course I knew, how could I not have known? It was as clear as daylight now, everything clicked into place. The phrase about being overdue he had used so casually the first night I had told him I was pregnant, that had niggled so much at the time. The times he had been away, the evasiveness with which he answered questions, his reluctance to admit our child was his, his refusal to give me money. Any blind person could see it all so clearly, except me.

'You knew he was married all this time,' I said to Bill, 'and yet you never even mentioned it; and I thought you were a friend — Christ, what kind of people are you?'

He looked shamefaced, but pressed on, talking quickly and earnestly. The best thing for me to do was to ring Eric's wife, tell her that I was expecting a baby, and ask for some money. She would have to give it to me, they had lots of money, she was only staying here for two weeks . . .

'Bill,' I interrupted him in mid-sentence, 'I thought you were Eric's friend. Why do you want to do this to him?'

'He's got it coming to him. It's time she knew about Eric. It's time she took him away from here. He doesn't fit in. At work, I mean. He doesn't get on with the rest of us . . .'

Bill was grasping my arm, kneading my hand, looking earnestly into my face to make me understand his sincerity and the importance of what he was saying. My mind was doing its usual flip — he continued talking, impressing on me the need to make Eric pay for what he had done by telling his wife. The fact that I was staring at him intently made him press home his argument even more. I couldn't take my eyes off him. This man had known that I was practically living with Eric for six months before I became pregnant, he had known Eric was married, he must have known that I didn't know. He was supposedly my friend, he was supposedly Eric's friend, yet he was now trying to use me for his own ends, by hurting another woman. The longer I stared at him, the more earnest he became, the more he reiterated how he was helping me, how much money I would be able to get from him.

While he talked my face was working as if any minute I was about to burst into tears. As far as I could remember I had never spat at anybody since I was a child, but now I had gathered a mouthful of saliva and I shot it at him with all the accuracy of an All-Ireland Champion. The glob of spittle landed right on his nose and I watched it slip slowly towards his left eye, his face crumpling in disbelief. The pain and frustration inside me were threatening to break loose in total hysteria, but I pushed them down and struck his face with my closed fist, hardly making a sound. Then I went back to my own car.

Joan came out of her house as soon as she saw me getting into my own car.

'Well?' she said with a 'let's have it all' expression on her face.

'Eric is married,' I said in a dead voice. 'That bastard wants me to tell his wife I'm pregnant and that he is the father. His wife is here in town at the moment and he thinks I should ring her with the good news. Can you imagine, I could easily have gone to the flat and that woman could have been there — dear Jesus what would I have done? That fucking bastard, he should have his balls cut off and hung on his forehead! I swear that married men should be branded, across the forehead with a branding iron, so that everyone can see them. Then if they become free again a line could be put through it like they do with road signs, because they are rotten, lying, sneaking, scheming fuckers, who have no thought for anyone only where to stick their pricks.' I was completely out of breath.

'Are you going to ring his wife?' Joan asked.

'For Christ's sake, of course I'm not,' I answered. 'What on earth good would come from my telling her?'

'Well, at least she might be able to get you some money . . . '

'Money, fucking money, because I'm short of money another woman is to have her life destroyed — ah no, we'll manage the money somehow, but I'm not going to be the cause of her misery. Maybe there are even more women! My God, how many brothers and sisters will my child have? Jesus, when they are fourteen, men should have their pricks tied in knots that would only be opened when they have sworn before a judge and jury that they would be responsible for what they would do with them!'

I went home apparently fairly in control and un-emotional, but the minute I got in my own door I broke down in an orgy of self pity and recrimination. After all, I was the one who could smell a married man a mile away. I was the cynic who couldn't ever really believe other women when they got involved unknowingly with married men. I thought about the night I had told Eric I was pregnant. It was the whole knowing way he had handled it that had bothered me at the time, but I hadn't been able to put it into context. What really drove me mad was the fact that he must have discussed it with his buddies at work — the fact that I was pregnant was public property and I desperately trying to keep it such a secret.

Bitterness spewed into my mouth with a poisonous taste. There was no justice. It was all right for Eric to have a wife and God knows how many other women and to have at least one of them pregnant, and to be able to wash his hands completely, take no responsibility, get no censure from society, while my life on the other hand was in chaos. I couldn't take it any more, I decided, I wouldn't, I'd ring his wife and tell her, why should I care? At least he would have to suffer too. The contemplation of my revenge gave me a warm glow of satisfaction, I'd make him squirm, I'd make him pay, then maybe he'd have some idea of how I felt, used and abused as though I had been thrown into a heap of slime and danced on, as though I would never be able to stand up straight again . . .

A few days later, I waited in the solicitor's office and finally Mr. Burke was free to see me.

'No, he didn't turn up for the meeting,' he answered in reply to my question. I hadn't expected him to really. For once I couldn't hide the depression and also a feeling of guilt, as if the whole situation was somehow of my making, as if I should have known all about Eric. But how could I? I told Mr. Burke that he had been right and that my doctor had been right — Eric was married. I also confessed that for a while I had contemplated telling

Eric's wife, but that I felt it would be a mean thing to do. He agreed that it would, and immediately my suspicion flared. Why did he think that? Who was he trying to protect? Did he have a wife too and run around with other women? He was only trying to protect another man.

I was being ridiculous, I knew, but all men, as far as I was concerned, were tarred with the same brush.

Nothing would lift the depression. The feeling that I had been taken in like an eighteen-year-old school kid made me feel bitter and angry with myself, also the realisation that somewhere at the back of my mind I must have kept the idea of marrying Eric as a final escape-hatch, and knowing now that it had never even been a possibility made me feel an even bigger fool. I fell deeper and deeper into a morass of dejection until one day Joan and I lay out in the dunes at Portmarnock, toying again with the possibility of me pretending I was married and how I could pass it off in the office. At last Joan said,

'Think of it like this, Aileen comes home a lot on her own when her husband is away, and nobody would really know whether she was married or not if she was pregnant.'

'All very well, Joan, but she is married, she has the bit of paper.'

'Yes, but after you came back to the office when the baby arrives, you could say you got married in England during the holidays.'

'OK, and where would I say this mysterious husband was?'

'You could say he was on a deep sea ship, like Aileen's husband, and that he didn't come home very often.'

'But when he never comes home at all, what will I say then?'

'Well you could say . . . ' Joan seemed to be stuck for an answer, but only for a second. 'You could say he fell over-board and was lost at sea.'

'Better still, I could say he was swallowed by a whale!'

'That's right,' she said with such a serious face that I couldn't help laughing. 'And then after a few years, if you did get married, you could say that the whale had thrown him up again like Jonah . . . '

We laughed so much that I began to cheer up again.

XXII

At last the office closed for the holidays. The relief was great. As far as Susan and I knew, nobody there suspected I was pregnant and presumably now I wouldn't be going back until after the baby was born. Susan, Betty and Joan disappeared on holidays, Susan with her family to Switzerland, Betty to Donegal, and Joan, who had arranged her holidays for this time before she changed jobs, off to Spain.

For the first few days I didn't realise how alone I was, but as the week progressed it dawned on me that I had no one to talk to, no one to visit and nowhere to go. The weather was boiling, the caravan was like a furnace. I became convinced that the neighbours were watching me, that someone had guessed I was pregnant. What would they do? Would they run me off the caravan site? At night when it was dark I went out, driving aimlessly around town, buying whatever food I needed, reading long into the night, staying in bed as long as possible during the day and feeling so much in need of sex, I thought I was going mad.

Several times I went to see my doctor, at least he was someone to talk to. I contemplated him, even fantasised about seducing him. Sometimes in the caravan, in my half-asleep fantasies, I had orgies with him and with Eric, and with men I didn't even know. Was I so sexy because of the heat? or being pregnant, or just damn loneliness?

I had visions of big hard long pricks, that I could stick into me and hold and pull. Orgasms brought temporary relief, but did nothing to stop the desperate need for something solid in between my legs.

By the end of the first week I was drifting into a state of total unreality, a half-world of sexual fantasy and a morbid belief that my neighbours were watching every move I made, and a desperate need for someone to talk to. On the few occasions when I actually did go out during the day, it took me an hour or more to get myself from the house to the car. As soon as I would go to open the door, I'd decide that someone was bound to see me and go back into the caravan again. Peeping from behind the curtains in the front room, staring at myself in the full length mirror, trying to make up my mind whether or not I looked pregnant, back to the window again, wondering were other people peering from behind their curtains waiting for me to go out, usually by the time I got to the car I was a nervous wreck.

It became clear that I had better do something with myself fast or I was going to become completely crazy. Also that I would have to go back to work as soon as the holidays were over, bump or no bump. I couldn't stand being alone for another six weeks which was when the baby was due. I went into town and bought two lots of materials and patterns for maternity dresses. They would look odd I knew, because the fashions that year were skinny, tight, poured into everything.

I had never been much use with a needle, but I cut out the patterns with care, pinned them, fitted them, tacked and finally hand-sewed every seam with meticulous precision. One was black plain material hanging in gathers from a straight yoke, the other was a light green, tiny print, cut in panels which hung from the shoulders. I got quite excited about making them, got myself out of bed early every morning and had a purpose for the day. I still went out mostly at night, but instead of driving hopelessly around I went up the mountains and walked for exercise. So I forgot about my fanny. The dresses turned out very well and I was thrilled. I convinced myself that in either one of them no one would have any idea that I was pregnant.

By the time the dresses were ready, Susan and her mother and sister were due home. I went out at eight o'clock in the morning to meet the boat. Having them back was an incredible joy. As soon as I had driven them home and heard all about Switzerland I dragged Susan away with me. Her mother and sister knew, she told me. They had felt for ages that there was something wrong with me and had tackled her on it. My mouth was dry with fear. 'What did they say?'

'Oh, for heaven's sake,' Susan said, fed up with my eternal pre-occupation with what people were saying about me. 'They are completely supportive and will give you any help you want — now shut up about it.'

'I'm going back to work next week,' I told her, knowing in advance that she was going to get mad. I was right, but she got angrier than I had expected.

'You can't go back, you'll be spotted, you are out now, stay out, you will never get away with it any longer!'

'I don't care,' I shouted back at her, 'I must go back, you haven't been locked up here for two weeks on your own, I'm nearly gone daft. And besides, if I wear another tight roll-on over the maternity one and stuff a huge bra with cotton wool, I'll still have a shape, please, Susan.' I pleaded with her. I'd go back anyway, but without her support I'd never survive.

'Oh, all right,' she gave in grudgingly.

The extra support of Susan's family was marvellous. It wasn't that they said anything much, but all the time I was in their house I felt secure and protected.

Susan's sister-in-law Sheila had gone into hospital. She went in during the night and had twin boys and the next day Susan and I met her husband Tom outside the hospital, to go in and see her and the twins. I felt guilty about meeting him because it had been so long since I had seen them. Neither he nor his wife knew I was pregnant and several months earlier I had given up seeing them because I couldn't stand the talk about their coming babies, and the preparations that were being made, and the things they were buying for them. However, that day, as we went up the hospital steps to the ward, our arms piled high with flowers and cards and boxes of chocolates, I knew Tom wasn't really mad with me, and in the joy of the moment didn't give two damns.

We went into the ward. Sheila wasn't there and after a few minutes a young nurse told us she had been moved to the top floor, ward four. Tom bounded up the stairs, Susan following and me bringing up the rear as best I could. As the three of us rounded into the ward, we con- certina'd into each other because Tom had stopped dead in the doorway. A barely recognisable Sheila was there, with tubes hanging from every part of her, a pale twisted face, the eyes closed. Before one of us could say anything, a nurse appeared and unceremoniously bundled the three of us out the door, told Susan and me to leave, and ordered Tom to wait for the doctor.

We left him there, staring back at him as we went down the stairs, terrified of what was happening, but not daring to voice a word. We sat in a corridor, waiting, the bundles of flowers on our laps, without a word. For ages we sat, silent, dumb, painfully waiting, waiting. At last Tom came down the stairs. 'They think she is safe,' he said. 'Let's get home.'

Together we turned, down the stairs, along the corridors, out into the afternoon. The city buzzed around us, traffic streamed past, the sun shone, people hurried in all directions and we were in our island of pain, unnoticed by everyone.

We walked up to the house, asking no questions, waiting until Tom chose to tell us what had happened. With a cup of coffee in his hand the words finally came, slow and dead. When he had left the hospital at two a.m., Sheila and the twins had been fine. At some time later it was discovered that she was bleeding internally where she had been badly torn. Doctors had fought most of the night and at one time it had seemed that the bleeding could not be stopped, and even when they had stopped it, it was still touch-and-go. But now she would pull through they said and Tom could go back in a few hours.

There was so little we could say. Tom was sick with the knowledge that his wife had nearly died in the night and the hospital hadn't even sent for him. We thrashed it around from one to another, trying at least to work up a fury against the hospital, but it was no good. She was safe, and we each dealt with the realization that she had been so near death.

'Why don't the three of you go out for a walk somewhere?' Susan's mother said, 'at least it would be better than sitting around here.'

We drove to Howth and walked on the headland. Terror for myself hit me, what would happen to me? If Sheila was in any other hospital, Tom said, she wouldn't have lived. Where was I going? What would happen to my baby if I died? Who would mind it? Would it never know its mother either? We sat on the side of the cliff, letting the sun warm us. There was only a tiny breeze, the air was clear and we could see straight across the bay to Dunlaoire harbour, ships passing slowly, the lighthouse down below us gleaming white, blue sky, blue sea.

XXIII

A few days later I called in to Edith and found a letter from my aunt saying that she would be at the airport at six o'clock that day, and if I could would I meet her. It was nine o'clock when I got the letter, so I had missed her. She had called, Edith said, with her priest and they had gone off to find someplace to stay for the night and would come back tomorrow at five for tea, in the hope that I might be there.

Edith was still getting my post and keeping it for me, and she insisted that if I would only give her a proper address, she would forward it to me, but I didn't want her to know about where I was living, so I kept telling her lies, half the time not being able to remember what I had told her before. I promised her that I would come for tea the next day. I felt quite secure with Edith, she wouldn't really notice me. It was only if I happened to bump into 'Upstairs' that I'd never escape. In the office the next morning I tormented Susan discussing the pros and cons with her. Should I see my aunt? Should I let her come and stay with me like she always did? Would she know I was pregnant? Jane would have fits, if I let my aunt find out. In the end Susan's patience broke.

'Go and meet your aunt this evening,' she said, 'And if she wants to stay let her, and if she finds out what do you care? It is your house and she didn't help you very much when you needed it, so stop worrying about her.' On the promise that Susan would come to tea too and stay the night, I decided to chance it.

My aunt and Father Mark were there when we arrived at Edith's. The table was set for tea, with all the best silver and china and faded linen napkins. The shabbiness of the huge room disappeared in the face of the charm with which Edith made us welcome and the style with which she served boiled eggs and slightly stale buttered bread, with strawberry jam. To listen to her chattering was a tonic, she was happy as a child at having so many visitors. In Edith's day, as she always said, there were proper procedures for entertaining and she always adhered to them. The formula for conversation was well laid out and recognised. For this tea time, it was a welcome by Edith to everyone, then the health of everyone present, plus their immediate families and friends, the weather, past, present and expected, destinations and lengths of stay of people going on holidays, and then the floor was open to general conversation.

I parked myself in a huge arm chair and let the conversation swirl and eddy around me, trying to stifle the pain when Edith lamented on how much she missed me, Susan trying to save me by laughingly assuring her that she was well rid of me. Susan knew that I was under awful strain in case there was a tap on the door and the familiar voice said: 'Are you there Mrs. K., may I come in?' Even if 'Upstairs' didn't spot my condition, the questions would go on forever. Father Mark had an appointment at eight and that gave us our excuse to leave. We offered to drop him off on our way. Leaving Edith I hugged her hard, knowing I wouldn't see her again for a while and telling her fifty more lies about going on holidays and so on.

My aunt admired the caravan and agreed that it was a good idea not to throw money away any longer on flats, no comment on why Edith didn't know where I was living, no indication that anything was out of the ordinary. We made coffee and talked. I explained that I couldn't drive her to the country because my car was in such bad shape. She said that was fine, that she would get the bus.

I knew she felt bad about not giving me the money when I asked her for it, but that was her problem, she had had her opportunity. She went off to bed and I promised to follow her shortly.

Among the letters I had brought home was one from my brother Dave in Belfast, saying he and his wife Threasa and their year-old baby, Billy, were coming down on Saturday and if I could put them up they would stay for a while. I handed the letter to Susan. I couldn't let him find out, I'd been warned not to tell him, and yet it would be so great to have him here.

'Oh fuck, Susan, what will I do?'

'Let him come, and if he doesn't like it he can lump it, he doesn't have to stay. I don't know why you worry so much about your family, I never see any of them doing anything for you.' Susan was getting more and more fed up with me and my family, and I couldn't blame her, but I wrung another promise from her to be with me when I met Dave and Threasa on Saturday. We concocted a letter telling him I had changed digs and to meet me outside a pub on the Belfast Road at 2 o'clock on Saturday, because he would never find the new place on his own.

In the excitement of Dave's letter we had forgotten all about my aunt, and we whispered about whether or not she knew — we couldn't decide whether she did or not. She was bound to find out when I went into bed.

But she didn't. I drove her to the bus next day and she made no sign that she knew I was pregnant or that I might have problems. There is nothing like good old family support, I thought. Did she really not know, or was it that she didn't want to know?

On the Saturday we sat outside the Coachman's Inn. Susan was in great form because in the space of a few days Sheila had improved so much. All the tubes had been removed, she was sitting up in bed, the colour was back in her face and she was beginning to feel good. Dave's car pulled in behind us, I looked at Susan and resisted the urge to ask her if I was noticeable, went back to the other car and told them to follow us. When they had looked around the caravan, their excitement and appreciation was fantastic, and made me feel that it was a stroke of genius on my part to have acquired it.

Susan and Dave went out to the sitting-room leaving Threasa and me in the bedroom. I waited with my breath held for her to say something, but she just continued chattering about how great the place was. A few minutes previously it had dawned on me that she was as pregnant as I was, if not more so. I had to interrupt her.

'Threasa, do you realise that I am pregnant?'

'It's just occurred to me this minute,' she said, 'You won't be getting married, then?'

'No.'

'When are you due?' There were tears standing in her eyes.

'About five or six weeks, I think, what about you?'

'Good God, maybe we'll have them together!' she laughed, 'I'm due around the end of next month too.'

'Threasa, how am I going to tell Dave?'

'Never mind Dave, I'll go and tell him, he'll be all right, don't you worry.' And off she went.

I sat in the bedroom and watched them both go out to the car and start bringing things in. I knew she was telling him. Finally I went out to the sitting-room and to break the awkwardness said,

'Dave, I'm sorry about this.'

I'll never forget his answer: 'Yerra, divil a bit sorry should you be — the more the merrier.' I couldn't take it. I ran back to the bedroom, shut the door and sobbed my heart out. I was completely overwhelmed by the simple acceptance of the situation, yet my brother and his wife hadn't the vaguest notion of what it meant to me. To be accepted by one of the family with no criticism, to know that my child would have an uncle and aunt and cousins like any ordinary child.

After sorting out their luggage, we cooked a big meal. Since I had been about two months pregnant, I had given up using salt, potatoes, bread, booze and cigarettes, except for odd occasions. I lived on a diet of hard boiled eggs, leaves of lettuce, tomatoes, some lean meat and milk; the things I missed most were potatoes and lots of salt. That evening Threasa turned out a pot of spuds in the middle of the table that would do justice to a harvest dinner, big floury potatoes with the skin just broken, dabbed with butter, lovely bacon and cabbage. I ate until I nearly burst, it was so good. We talked about the babies, what we had bought for them, and on hearing that I had nothing yet for mine, Threasa insisted that we must go into town and get things immediately. I loved it, making plans for my baby as if it was the most natural thing in the world.

I went back to work the following Monday. Tied into two roll-ons and with my forty-two-inch bra stuffed hard with cotton wool, I convinced myself that I was the shapeliest thing in sight. I wore the black dress, sewn by my own hands. God knows how it stayed together, but it certainly covered me up. Susan was in despair, swore that I'd ruin everything just so near the end. I'd be bound to be caught she said, and not only would I be sacked, but I'd get no unemployment or anything. I was mad, she said for the twentieth time.

It was a terrible chance, and I couldn't make Susan understand that I just had to be at work. I begged her not to desert me, and she got angry all over again that I should even dare suggest such a thing. We took extra precautions going in and out of the office, she nearly always in front of me, the huge cardigan around my shoulders, the basket in front of me, the two corsets holding my belly in and the stuffed bra sticking my chest out. We were very busy in the office. The bank strike continued, and cash for salaries and wages was a constant problem, but trying to keep our foreign payments up to date was even worse. However, the more problems we had, the less time anyone had to pay attention to anyone else.

Going home in the evenings was fantastic. I didn't care about the neighbours, or whether they were looking at me. I walked boldly in and out to the car. The dinner was always on the table and I couldn't resist the food. Sometimes we went for a drive in the evenings, Dave driving while Threasa and I flopped in the car like two grounded seals. Dave joked and laughed about the size of the two of us, we compared signs and symptoms, we enjoyed ourselves and I was content. Several nights I baby-sat their year old son, while they went out on their own for a drink or to a show.

On the Saturday Dave and Threasa went back to Belfast. The 'troubles' in the North were escalating again, and they were not happy about going back. I felt alone again and unprotected, yet if things got very bad, I consoled myself, I could go up and stay with them. I didn't know what problems that was supposed to solve, but I kept it in my head as some kind of escape.

XXIV

Since discovering that Eric was married, Mr. Burke had sent him several more letters, none of which was answered. I had said that I would go and talk to Eric before we took any more drastic action, but the idea didn't really appeal to me and I had kept putting it off while Dave and Threasa were around. They had never once questioned me about my child's father. When I was on my own again I thought I had better go and see him and get it over with. It wasn't as if I desperately needed the money; as long as the banks stayed closed I just got more and more into debt. Still, if he gave me even a hundred pounds it would pay for the nursing home and I could buy a few things. Far more than the money, I had a fierce need for him to acknowledge his child. It seemed to me that he must do this or I could never survive.

My plan was simple. If Eric's car was outside his door I'd give my signal, and presumably if his wife was still around the door wouldn't be opened. I was pleased to discover that after all I didn't seem to be particularly worried. I was perfectly calm. If he was there well and good, if not I'd probably feel relieved at avoiding the confrontation for another while. He was there. As soon as I got into the flat I didn't feel quite so detached. The familiar smells, the soft lights, the eternal music! All the old destructive memories started tearing at me.

'Good to see you,' Eric said, putting his arm around me

and giving me a brief kiss, 'Give me your coat.' Je-sus! Just when one wanted to deal on a particular level the ground was taken from under one's feet. My temper started rising. I didn't want any physical or emotional contact with him. I didn't want any argument. I just wanted to state factually that if he didn't go and see my solicitor and sort this whole business out, then I was taking him to court.

'Have a drink,' he said, pouring me a brandy without waiting for an answer.

'No thanks, I'm not drinking.'

'Have a cigarette then.'

'No, I'm not smoking either. Eric, I just came to say that either you must give me some money and admit this child is yours, or I am taking you to court. I honestly do not want to argue with you or anything, I just want to tell you.'

'Money!' He snorted contemptuously, 'I have no money. How much do you need anyway?'

'Sixty pounds, a hundred pounds.' My hopes rose. He seemed suddenly more easy, almost interested. Maybe he would just give me the bloody money and a letter to the solicitor saying the child was his and I could get to hell out of the place and tell the child forever that its father was great and provided for it. But then he practically spat:

'I haven't got any money. And I've got enough problems without you. When my wife was here someone rang her and told her I had a woman pregnant. She came down to the job and challenged me with it. But I was too smart, I said to her, who told you those lies? A man. A man, I said, don't you understand someone here has it in for me, they want to get me out. You ask them, I said to her, you ask them where is this bloody woman, produce this woman – they can't.' He was gloating, completely carried away by his ability to deceive people. 'I warned Bill – you know Bill – I warned him, they want to get rid of me . . .'

I finally exploded, 'You blithering fool, it was your

precious Bill who rang your wife! You haven't even got one friend!' I couldn't help rubbing it in. 'You poor half-wit! Your buddy Bill even came to me first to try to get me to ring your wife — your wife that I didn't even know existed — you stinking, lousy creepy crawly, they hate you so much on that job that they would do anything to get rid of you. I wouldn't tell your wife, but that bastard obviously did. There isn't the makings of a decent bone between the whole lot of you.'

At first he didn't believe what I was saying, but then I could see the pieces falling into place in his head. He walked around the room, taking deep pulls of his cigarette. At last he came back to where I was standing with my back against the fridge. And then another change took place. He held both my arms; all the old charm, that I once found sexy, but now considered greasy smarm, crept back over his face.

'Of course it was Bill,' he purred. 'He's next in line for my job. I knew you wouldn't let me down. I'll make it up to you. Christ, I'll fix Bill, they won't get rid of me that easily. Listen, why don't you ring my boss and tell him that it's all just lies about me, that you're the woman who is supposed to be pregnant and you're not up the pole at all. Yeah, why don't you tell him what Bill did behind my back — how he tried to get you to ring my wife. Will you do that for me — for our child?'

My temper had risen to boiling point, but had disappeared again at the total incongruity of the whole scene. The man was crazy, the whole situation was crazy. I laughed at him, derisive, cutting. He looked at me suspiciously, not sure about my reaction. He paced the room again, worried, completely absorbed in this new aspect of his own predicament.

Coaxingly I said, 'I'll tell you what, give me some money now and a letter for the solicitor and I will go away, and I promise I'll never come near you again. Even fifty quid will do, it will pay for the nursing home at least. Please?' He answered as if he was talking to a silly child who wouldn't stop bothering him.

'I can't, I haven't got the cash just at the moment, I have to pay seventy pounds for a new suit on Friday night . . .'

It was then that something broke inside in me. All my blood drained away somewhere, I became icy cold, my breath stopped, nothing moved in my body, my mind was crystal clear. I knew what I was going to do. I was going to kill Eric. It was the best thing. He had humiliated me beyond endurance. This was the last straw. He'd be better away where he couldn't do any more damage. It was quite simple. He was still talking about his new suit, how the tailor was the most expensive in Dublin. I was standing with my back to the fridge. On the chopping board on top of it he kept his meat and vegetable knives. I just had to reach back and take one, any one would do, they were all strong and sharp. I moved slightly away from the fridge towards him, somehow forcing my lips apart so that I seemed to be smiling. I would plunge the knife in, just above the top of his belly, that would do it. I slid my hand along the top of the fridge behind me, he was moving closer, all the old charm coming on again. My hand wasn't finding the knife, I moved back to stretch and something in my face warned him — for an instant I could see horror on his face as he stood there petrified — in desperation I turned to grab the knife — there was none, there was no knife.

The icyness disappeared, my body started getting warm, the baby kicked. Eric moved back from me as if in a slow motion movie. I began to crumble, I was trying to say something, but no sound would come out of my mouth.

I drove blindly down to the sea at the Bull Wall. I left the car and hurled myself into the long grass of the dunes. At first the pain wouldn't come out of me, but gradually my cries grew louder, I grovelled in the sand. I had intended to kill him . . . I would have killed my child's father . . . would have been sent to jail . . . my baby would have been born in jail . . . for that I would never forgive him . . . never . . . he had nearly turned me into a murderer . . . nearly made me take a life. I had become so caught. up in his fantasies and intrigues and plots that I had lost all sense of proportion, all idea of the importance of things. I must never see him again, that was for sure. Nothing he could do for me in terms of money or giving my child a name would make up for the fact that I would have killed him . . . I would have killed him . . . my God, the screams gurgled out of my mouth and circled around my head, my child would have no father, nobody loved me. I rolled over on my back and yelled up at the sky. 'Somebody pity me, help me? there must be somebody somewhere to help me? God, couldn't You help me? No, of course You couldn't, You only help those who help themselves — You only play on safe bets. But then You are one of the boys too — aren't You?'

My guts began to heave, I writhed and groaned, spewing up everything I had eaten and when there was nothing left convulsing my body with empty retching. I lay there thinking about my poor baby, would it ever survive? what would happen? . . . The sun was edging up over the horizon when I woke, the predawn air was clean and fresh, waves lapped gently, the world was cleansed, starting again, a new day. Could I ever start again, I wondered, would anything ever cleanse me? drag me up from the humiliation and degradation? Would I ever lift my head again? — could anyone as used and abused as I was, ever be anything but a door mat?

PART THREE

XXV

I agreed with Betty's sister Bernie that she would look after the baby for three pounds a week. I would deliver the child with nappies and bottles in the morning and collect it in the evening. In another two weeks at the most 'it' would be someone, a squealing boy or girl. My doctor was positive it would be a boy.

Getting into bed I felt very peculiar — muzzy and strange, uneasy somehow. I thought I might be going into labour. Next morning I was worse. I felt very ill, but couldn't quite pin it down, my whole body seemed to be in revolt, but I wasn't having what I imagined to be labour pains. I dragged myself out of bed and started to get dressed. I had closed my bra and was stuffing back the cottonwool that had fallen out when it occurred to me that right under the line of my bra was hurting like hell. All around my body were little red spots. I felt all hot and sticky and in pain. I decided I had better call in to my doctor on my way to work; it was very early, but I knew he would see me if he was there. I had barely said I had spots under my breasts when he lifted up my bra and grunted.

'That's it, me girl, that's you out of that office at long last — you've got shingles, you are to go home immediately — here is a sick cert.'

'I can't go home,' I interrupted him, 'I must go to work.'

'Listen, child, do you understand that you are very sick? — You are running a high temperature. I cannot give you any medication for it because you are pregnant, so you are going to have to put up with the pain. Now go home and go to bed. Have you anyone out in that place to look after you?'

'Yes, I'll be fine . . . '

'You *won't* be fine!' he nearly roared at me, 'You don't know what you are talking about, you need taking care of. This will probably bring on the baby early — go home and get to bed and I will be out this afternoon to see you.' He practically shoved me out the door.

I went straight to the office and sat behind my desk, not even having the energy to take off my coat. Before I could ring Susan to tell her, my boss came down with some papers for me. He was in great form and had nearly gone out the door again before I could force myself to say,

'By the way, I'm going home, I'm sick.'

'Good heavens! You do look a bit washy, what's wrong with you?'

'I've got shingles, the doctor says I must go home to bed.'

'Shingles!' he exclaimed in amazement, 'God help you, they are frightful things, you're going to be sick for a long time.' And then in a puzzled voice, 'People only get shingles from worrying, what on earth have you got to worry about?'

I sat there, my head propped on my elbows, my fatherless child hidden under the desk — perspiration pouring out of every pore in my body, the pain above my waist suddenly searing through me like red hot knives. I looked at him and said in as conversational a tone as I could muster, 'I don't understand it either — what on earth could be worrying me?'

'Do you want me to drive you home, or get one of the lads to do it?'

'Oh Jesus, no! Honestly, I'll be fine, thanks all the same.'

'Well go home now, and don't come back until you're feeling better. You are in for a bad time. If there is anything you want us to do, let us know.' He went away shaking his head in sympathy.

Two minutes later Susan was in the door. 'What on earth is the matter? His Nibs says you've got shingles?'

'I have. I'd better get out of here fast, I feel very ill.'

'Hold on, and someone will drive you.'

'No, I'll make it home, I think it's better to take the car, I might need it. The wages are all there ready for handing out. Come out as soon as you can.'

The road and the traffic kept weaving and moving in all kinds of strange directions as I drove home, but I made it safely into the caravan. That was it, I figured, one way or another I was there until the baby came. The relief of getting out of my clothes, particularly the bra and roll-ons, was great. I felt very light-headed and realised that I would have to have help in case the baby started coming suddenly. The only people with whom I had become friendly on the site were Áine and Liam, who lived in the big caravan beside me. From the beginning I felt there was no intrusion in their friendship and yet there was an openness about them which I did not feel in my brief encounters with other neighbours. I often wondered if they guessed that I was pregnant, but they never gave any sign of having done so. I waited until I saw Áine in her kitchen and made signs for her to come over when she could.

It was about half an hour before she arrived.

'Sorry for being so long,' she said, 'But I had to wait until the little fellow fell asleep. What's wrong? Why are you home at this time of the day? You look awful.'

Áine, I've got shingles,' I said, 'I must go to bed. Áine, did you realise that I am pregnant?'

'I can't help noticing you now,' she answered with surprise. 'How far gone are you?'

'The baby is due any time, can't you see?'

'My God! I don't believe it! Do you mean to say? No, it can't be. You mean you've been going around all this time pregnant and I haven't noticed you? Well you are some woman. Christ, get into bed quick.' She caught me as I swayed towards her.

It was good to be lying down. I didn't care about anything anymore, Áine sat on the side of the bed. There must be questions she wanted to ask me, I knew, but she was afraid of offending me.

'It's all right,' I smiled at her, 'Ask me anything you like.'

'Are you going to keep the baby?'

'Yes, I'm going to keep it.' I wasn't up to any further explanation and she didn't seem to need it.

'What about the . . . ?

'The father? Oh, he is not very much help just now, I don't expect to see him again.'

She sat there with me, every now and again marvelling that I had managed to escape her notice. She had to leave to get her husband's lunch, promising to be back again when she could. Sometime in the afternoon the doctor came, letting himself in without any ceremony. When I tried to lift my nightdress to show him the shingles, several bits of it had become stuck to what were now open sores. The pain was terrible.

'Look,' he said, 'The only thing I can do is powder them to try and dry them up, but you had better leave off that nightdress, there is no point in getting that stuck to them and having to drag it off. I won't be out to see you for several days. The pain will get very bad. Take some aspirin and get someone to powder you a few times a day. Have you someone to look after you?' If he asked me that question again I'd scream at him.

'Yes, yes, I have, one of the girls is coming to stay with me,' I lied to stop him being anxious about me.

'Good. Now, that baby will probably come early. The minute you get any pains, go into the nursing home — you know where it is, don't you? — and get them to ring me. Now, try to get some rest, you will be all right; have you plenty of books?'

'Yes,' I answered, 'I have lots of books, I'll be grand now.' I was anxious to get rid of him and not have him ask me any more questions. I didn't actually know where the nursing home was. It was somewhere on Hatch Street, but that was all I knew. He had told me several times to ring them, to get whatever information I needed about what I should bring in. He had booked me in there himself. I had promised that I would ring, but could never bring myself to do it. I had a totally unreasoning fear that they would ask me all kinds of personal questions which I didn't want to answer. Maybe I also knew that it would be the final evidence that this thing was real and was going to happen. As long as I still didn't know where that nursing home was, it might just all go away or turn out to be a bad dream.

That evening Áine and Liam came and insisted that I must come and stay in their caravan with them, they had an extra bedroom and would look after me. I felt bad about refusing, but in the end made them understand that I would be easier where I was; as long as they would come in and out I wouldn't be worried. With them to rely on I wouldn't be afraid if the baby started in a hurry.

A few days after I left the office, Betty arrived in a panic one morning. Another friend of ours had driven her and was out in the car, could she bring her in?

'Of course,' I said, and Norah was dragged in to what must have been one of the most confusing scenes she had ever encountered, and with no time to explain to her what it was all about. All that Betty wanted then were the keys to the office and the explaining could be done another time. They found them and the two rushed off, but in the afternoon Norah came back to tell me what had happened.

Apparently His Nibs had arrived in the office that morning, and suddenly realised that I had in fact performed a function there, that I still had the keys to the safe, and that I had better be replaced while I was ill. The replacement was simple — an accountant was brought in from our auditing company — but the keys had to be collected. He had strolled into Susan's office and said, 'I'll drive you around to Brig's flat, and you can pick up the keys.'

Susan, in a panic, had stuttered that I was staying at Betty's while I was ill. He said fine, they would go over there. Susan assured him that Betty wouldn't be in at that time of the day and that she would have to find out what time she would be there. As soon as she got the boss out of the way, Susan had rung Betty, who luckily had been at home because her car had broken down. Susan had cryptically told Betty to get the keys from me and have them at her house at two o'clock, and then put down the phone, without waiting to find out that Betty had no car. The only one Betty could think of to help was Norah who lived around the corner from her, so she had dashed in to Norah's kitchen when she was in the middle of getting the lunch and dragged her off on the mystery tour, promising to tell her later what it was all about. They had had to ask Norah's neighbour to come in and keep an eye on the baby and then the two of them had driven frantically across town, grabbed the keys, returned to Betty's, and when one of the men from the office called at two o'clock, the keys were there. I was supposedly upstairs asleep under heavy sedation, not to be disturbed, and everything was in order. If I had remembered to leave the keys in the office in the first place the crisis would not have arisen.

Susan came with Sheila and Tom. I couldn't believe Sheila was the same person that I had seen in the hospital. In such a short time she was blooming, and the twins were marvellous. Áine came every minute of the day she could spare. She fed me and powdered me and tried to keep me amused with gossip about people on the site. It was amazing the things that went on there that I never noticed. Liam managed a bar in town and on his way home every night he would knock at my window and ask, 'Are you all right, Brig. Anything you want?' If anything happened unexpectedly I just had to bang on the wall and they would hear it clearly. My doctor came every few days, always trying to be cheerful, assuring me the baby would come any day, warning me not to put water on the sores — as if I even had the energy — and promising me a fine bouncing baby boy.

I took all their kindness and support like a desert soaking up water, never able to tell them what it all meant to me, but I stored it inside me and it made me strong.

The days and nights meshed together in a haze of pain. The shingles after several days made a half circle of exposed nerve ends, stretching from the middle of my back to the centre of my breasts. If anything touched them I screamed. I could only lie on the tiny bit of my side that was clear and this became unbearable after half an hour or so. I could sit up but couldn't lean against anything. I walked around the caravan, but was too weak to stay on my feet for very long. One of the best positions I discovered was to kneel on the bed hunched over on my arm; this way I could sleep for short periods. During the days I took the few aspirin I allowed myself, and they eased the pain a little, so that I could talk to Áine or read, but in the nights I was insane.

One night it was so bad I started rocking over and back and eventually hitting my head against the wall, because it felt good. I had heard of people doing that, but it was because there was something wrong with them, they were mad, mad, mad, ha, ha, but so was I, and as well I was bad, bad, bad, and I must suffer, suffer, suffer, 'cause I was a woman, woman, woman and men ruled the world.

'But I didn't do it alone, I didn't fuck myself,' I cried, 'Why must only I suffer, a man did it with me . . . '

Because you were made by a man god, out of a man, for the use and benefit of men, you're a fool, you're a fool, you're a fool . . . men rule the world, they can fuck where they like, spill their seed and make babies, as long as there are women like you, 'cause you're a fool.'

'But it's not fair, I didn't want much from him, oh Christ, if only he was here to hold my hand and stop the pain . . . '

You're a fool, how can he be here, he has got to buy a new suit for seventy pounds, seventy pounds, seventy pounds . . . he has got other women to fuck, to fuck, to fuck, he has got other babies to make, to desert, to leave fatherless, he hasn't time to hold your hand, hold your hand, but he'd have time to fuck you. But you're not fuckable anymore. He must go away and fuck his other women, nothing can stop him because women are fools, they need men, women are nothing, they have no souls, no minds, so they trap men to find an identity, but men pay them back . . .'

But I screamed in the night: by Jesus I swear if I survive this, someone will pay me back, something will be done, because no woman should have to suffer like this to bring a child into the world. By propping cushions and pillows up against the wall, I was able to rest standing on my head — what a great way to be! — standing on my head, standing on my head, with my big fat belly sticking out, with my shingles all paining so that I was screaming, but it really didn't matter a damn, 'cause I was mad, mad, gloriously mad.

XXVI

At about seven o'clock one evening, Áine and I were in the bedroom chatting when there was an unusual knock on the door. She closed the bedroom door after her and went to answer it, and arrived back with my brother Eddie and his wife Grace, looking as though the sky had fallen down on them. My first reaction was why in the fuck couldn't people cheer up, but I was glad to see them. Áine stayed around long enough to give them tea and cake and then left with a lift of the eyebrows. I was annoyed with myself for feeling angry with them. I knew they were trying hard, that it had been an effort for them to come.

'Eddie, I'm sorry about this,' I said, as I had said to Dave, and because I could think of nothing more original to break the silence with.

'Oh well,' he answered with a deep sigh, 'It is your bed, you will have to lie on it.'

I tried to think of something appropriate to say in reply to this brotherly support, but if I opened my mouth the bitterness would spew out, so I shut up.

'You intend keeping the baby, according to Dave,' he continued helpfully. 'Have you any idea of what you are letting yourself in for? How difficult it is to rear a child with two people, let alone one? Wait until you are up all night and trying to work all day, I'm telling you, and wait until the baby starts teething, and gets sick and you have to take time off from work, then you will know — it won't be much fun.' He lit a cigarette. 'Ah well,' with another sigh which he dragged all the way up from his toes, 'I suppose you have to find these things out for yourself.'

The silence was painful. I got them talking about the caravan and asked Eddie if he would ever have a look at the television which was on the blink. That got rid of him for a while, and Grace and I relaxed. She knew exactly how I was feeling and told me to try not to mind Eddie, he was very concerned about me, but he had such a gift for saying the wrong thing. We chatted about how she and Eddie were getting on and about their children. They had been married fifteen years, with five lovely children, and they had been through all kinds of hell and yet they were somehow surviving. I had the greatest admiration for them, but had no way of communicating with my brother, always desperately wanting to relate to him in an ordinary way which by now I should have recognised as impossible.

They stayed for ages, she fairly relaxed, he tense and strained. They invited me to come down any time I wished, to come and stay when the baby was born. I promised I would, knowing I would have to be very badly off to endure my brother's painful efforts to make me feel comfortable. But I was grateful. The offer to have me and the baby down was made in the knowledge that it would cause a scandal in the small town where they lived, as well as giving them the problem of having to explain to their own children how their aunt had suddenly acquired a baby with not a husband in sight. It took courage, and I appreciated it, I knew the kindness was there, and I would have to learn to accept the fact that my brother and I would never be able to communicate at any but the most superficial level. But I was excited after they had left. My child would have five more cousins, as well as another aunt and uncle.

Slowly the sores dried up and the pain began to subside. Just being able to lie in comfort and read was ecstasy and I read everything I could lay my hands on. I got up for most of the day, though I still felt weak. I couldn't have a bath and washed standing at the sink, which reminded me of a rigmarole Edith used about washing, which began 'Wash down as far as possible' and went on 'Wash up as far as possible' and lastly 'Wash possible.' I knew she considered it a very risqué joke and would only tell it to selected friends. Anyway, those days I washed as much of 'possible' as I could reach under my belly. Thinking about Edith made me sad, as it always did now. She had rung the office looking for me and Susan had told her that I was very sick with shingles. Since then I had asked Susan to go around every few days and reassure her with bulletins of my improving condition. To keep her from trying to visit me Susan had told her that I was staying with my brother while I was sick.

There was no sign of the baby coming. While I was very sick I didn't care a damn, but as soon as I started getting better I began to worry. What if something was wrong? Was the baby alive? Why didn't it come? It was nearly three weeks since I had left the office and the doctor promised it would be early. Every night I expected to go into labour, but every day I felt better and stronger and began to feel that my bump would never disappear and that I would go on like that forever. Since I had left work it seemed to me that I had spread to twice my previous size and had put on so much weight that getting into any kind of clothes was really uncomfortable.

In the evenings once it got dark I went driving out around the mountains like a lunatic, looking for bumpy roads, because someone told me it was one way to get started. Another was to drink castor oil. Neither did a blind bit of good, but the oil nearly made me puke up my guts. I took to going up to Bernie's in the afternoons and sometimes at night. Necessity made strange bedfellows, I thought. Bernie was not the sort of person with whom I would naturally become very friendly. She was a whiner by nature and occupation, the exact opposite of her sister in every way. She was the youngest of Betty's sisters and had been spoiled rotten by all of them. Her mother, a wonderful woman in her late seventies, who looked about sixty-five and had reared thirteen children of her own, lived with Bernie and her family, and practically reared Bernie's children as well. It was very hard to see how she would survive without her mother. But she filled a very great need for me just then, and I began to spend a lot of time at her house.

Apart from being worried about the baby not coming, I was pretty content these days. I was feeling well, I had somebody organised to mind the baby, the banks were still closed so I had no need to worry about money, and I had come to some kind of terms with the fact that Eric would never play a father's role in my child's life. This had been the big bugbear. I was depriving my child of a father. I had led myself along with all kinds of carrots: maybe Eric and I would get together, maybe we would even get married, maybe he would come and visit, maybe he would write to the child, maybe, maybe, maybe — until the night I thought of killing him. Unlike my previous contemplation of suicide, there was no doubt in my mind that if the knife had been where it should have been, I would have stuck it in him. The realization of this had brought me to a total reassessment of the situation regarding Eric. I decided that I didn't want him as a father for my child. A person who could wheel and deal to the extent that he had, wasn't fit for the job. We were free of him and I was glad. The more I contemplated fathers in the context in which I knew them, the more I decided that they were a sorry lot and I came to the conclusion like Maisie Madigan about the 'Dublin Polis' — that fathers as fathers in this country is null and void.

So I was pretty content. I half liked the idea of being at home from work, a situation I had never been in before, pretending to be a housewife. Mostly I only saw Áine, but I loved talking to her and continued to be amazed by her tales of the 'carryings-on' on the site. It was hard to believe that so many dramas could be taking place in such a small community. It reminded me of a huge poster which one saw all over Ireland those days — an enormous bill board which said "All Human Life Is There." For years I had thought it was something to do with the Bible, until someone explained to me that it was an ad for the *News of the World*. Times change. Anyway I kept having fantasies of hanging one of these posters at the entrance to our site.

And then the peace was disrupted again. Áine thought that I was going into labour and was having some kind of convulsion into the bargain because I was jabbering like a mad monkey.

'No! No, no, it can't happen! I don't believe it, oh Christ no, anything but this!' Áine and I were in the front room drinking our eternal coffee, but she had her back to the window and didn't see my dear sister Jane's car pulling up outside. 'Jesus, Áine, please don't leave me alone with her.' I closed my eyes and hoped she would disappear, but she didn't.

She came in with her usual air of heroically subdued martyrdom and as quickly as she could Áine scuttled. The stilted conversation carried on until I was sure the tension was causing the shingles to start up again under my breasts.

'Eddie wrote and told me you had shingles, that must be terrible,' she said, in a voice that suggested it was just what I deserved.

'It was bad, but I'm fine now, I just wish the baby would hurry up and come.' Keep it light, I thought, make it casual, oh Jaysus, wrong tactic, her face was freezing over.

'Why did you tell Dave and Eddie? I thought I told you not to tell anyone.'

'I didn't exactly tell them. Dave and Threasa came on holidays as they always do and they found out. They told Eddie. They didn't take it too badly.'

'No, of course they don't have to bear the shame of it.'

Oh shit, what was that supposed to mean? Somehow I must divert her, I couldn't take the crucifixion she was determined I must go through for my sins.

'I wonder if you would ever do me a big favour,' I said

in my most placating voice. 'I must have a wedding ring going into the nursing home. I don't want to go into town in case anyone sees me, do you think you could possibly get one for me? Your hands are about the same size as mine, I could go into labour anytime and I do need it.'

She went off at last on her errand of mercy, which would keep her away for a few hours at least. I breathed a sigh of relief. God, what a misfortunate miserable bitch she was, why couldn't she just go home and mind her own business? Áine made signs from her kitchen window to know if she was gone for good, and I shouted in whispers from my side door that she was only gone into town and would be back shortly. And of course she was. In fairness to her she bought me a beautiful wedding ring. It cost four pounds, it was a wide smooth band and when I put it on my finger it nearly seemed as if it offered some kind of protection to me and my child. If only I could pretend now that I had a husband someplace.

'I suppose the father has run away on you. That is, if you ever knew who he was.'

She was warming up again. In a minute we were going to be in a tearing, screaming row. It was as if there were a whole lot of words inside in her that she just had to get out, and maybe if I let her say them it would be all over, but I didn't want to hear them, I didn't want to be beaten into the ground any further. She could shut her mouth or get to hell out of it. I knew my refusal to discuss anything with her was driving her daft, but I couldn't relent. What I sensed from her was what I had always sensed while I was growing up — the firm belief that I was totally irresponsible, that I couldn't care less about anyone but myself, that I had shamed the whole family, and that instead of being down on my belly crawling and covering my head in sackcloth and ashes, and apologising every five minutes for my very existence, I was living in the lap of luxury, with people supporting me and carrying on as if I was normal. The urge to tear her asunder was enormous and I kept thinking, 'if she doesn't get out of here soon I will take her apart, limb from limb.'

We were both saved by the arrival of Bernie in the door, to see why I hadn't been up that day. She had hoped it was because I had gone into hospital. Not in any way realising the hostility that was thick in the room, she rattled on about the baby and labour and the fact that it looked as though I would never move, and how big I was, and how incredible that no one had noticed at the office, what an ass I was to have bought so few things for the baby, and on and on, until I thought the whole place would blow apart.

Finally she got up to go, exclaiming about how lucky I was to have my sister with me and assuring me that I must surely go into labour that night. The minute the door was closed after her, I said 'I'm going to bed, I'm dreadfully tired,' and fled, getting into bed and putting out the light so fast that she didn't have a chance to come after me. I fell asleep and dreamt that I was living forever with a baby inside me that refused to be born, and a sister who refused to leave.

When I woke up and found that she was ready to go I was delighted, but then as she was nearly out the door I started crying. I was just as surprised as she was and I wasn't at all sure what it was about.

'What on earth are you crying for?' she asked, standing in the open doorway and talking back to me in the kitchen.

'I don't know, the baby is due anytime, and I thought you might stay until it came.'

'I can't stay. Anyway you have plenty of people to look after you.'

'I haven't, I haven't, I'm on my own, I've got no one to take me to the hospital if it comes in the middle of the night.' I was beginning to sob, to collapse completely, and then I could see the change in her face — I was going to grovel and beg and she was going to get her pound of flesh after all. Her face softened and she moved back into the caravan. But I had straightened up again and got control of my voice.

'It's all right, I'll be fine, people will look after me, don't worry.'

We stood staring at each other, both knowing we had lost our chance. We had burnt our bridges, there would never again be a way over the chasm.

'Your doctor will look after you.'

'That's right, he will.' She turned slowly down the steps and left. I heard the tyres crunch on the gravel as she turned the car and the sound of the engine died away up the road.

XXVII

It was four weeks since I had left the office and still no sign of the baby coming. The shingles had dried up completely, only red blotches all around, and still I wasn't allowed to have a bath. Odd darts of pain came and went like ghosts but otherwise I was feeling fine. I was so big it would have been easier for me to roll than walk. Every evening I went down to the village after dark to phone Susan and tell her I was still around. I drove around the mountains and swallowed more castor oil. Nothing did any good. In the evenings I usually called into Bernie's. Nobody came to visit, because they expected that every day I must be gone into hospital. I became an embarrassment to myself and the few people who were waiting for this child to be born.

At about seven o'clock on a Friday night I went down to the village and rang my doctor. I was desperate, I told him, he must have some idea when the baby would come.

'Please,' I begged into the phone, 'There must be something you can do to make it come, I need to get back to work soon.' That was the wrong thing to say.

'Babies will come when they are good and ready and not before. You cannot go back to work and that is all there is about it, so put it right out of your head. Your baby is bound to come in the next week.' I tried to tell him that I was not talking about going back to work before the baby came, but it seemed too much trouble.

'Thank you, doctor,' I said and put down the phone.

I drove up to Bernie's. Brian, her husband, wasn't home yet from work and she asked me to drive her to a shopping centre to do her Friday night shopping. Cornelscourt was the in place for shopping and we drove all the way across town and out to Stillorgan. The economics of driving such a distance because some items were marginally cheaper than at the local store, baffled me, but Cornelscourt it had to be. The attraction of the place also escaped me. As far as I was concerned it was sheer bedlam under one roof. So I trailed disconsolately after Bernie and her huge cart and tried in vain to look impressed when she exclaimed in raptures over some tin which was a penny or half a penny less than at some other store. The stupidity of coming out to such a place hit me after a few minutes. It was obvious that at least half of Dublin was trying to shop there and I was bound to meet someone I knew. I told Bernie that I would wait outside and went and sat in the dark comfort of the car.

It was ten o'clock by the time we got home and unloaded all the purchases and had coffee and discussed all the prices and the savings and how white the latest brand of washing powder made the children's nappies. Oh Christ, I thought, as I slammed the car into gear on my way home, I was fed up with fucking women and their shopping lists, and penny-saving and whiter than white nappies. Bernie had asked me to stay, but I preferred to go home to my own bed, I was much more comfortable there.

As usual I was sitting up reading late into the night, when it occurred to me that I had been to the loo about three times and was on the way again. I seemed to be piddling for ages. I got back into bed and took up my book again. Soon I was all wet. I got out of bed, put on two STs, moved over to the dry side of the bed and continued to read.

'You're in labour, I'm telling you you're in labour.'

'I'm not,' I studiously stuck to my book, 'fuck off now, it is two o'clock in the morning, I'm not in labour, that bloody baby wouldn't come all day, so it can wait now until morning... ' I continued to read with enormous concentration. Suddenly the whole bed was wringing wet, where did it all come from?

'From you, ye fool, the water is broken.'

Oh Jesus Christ, what did that mean, what did I know about labour? There should be pains, pains, I didn't have any pains, yes I did, little ones in my back, but they were nothing — still I had better call Áine. I pounded on the wall and waited, there wasn't a stir. I pounded again, why weren't they coming? I got out of bed and looked, their van was in pitch darkness, they had been leaving a light on for me every night. And then I remembered, of course, Áine had told me, they had gone away for the night. Since they knew I was pregnant they had stayed at home to be there in case I needed them, but since it had looked as though I was not going to move for another week or so they had gone down to Áine's home for the night and would be back sometime the next day. She had told me to make sure I had somebody else with me, but I had completely forgotten. 'What will I do now?' I asked out loud.

'Get dressed, you fool, and get yourself up to Bernie's.'

No need to panic, first babies never come in a hurry, they take ages, anyway women have babies in all kinds of places and without anybody around.

'What are you scared of then?'

'I don't know, but I'm bloody awful scared.'

I was dressed. What do I do next? Pack something in a bag: what? Nightdress, toothbrush, vest for baby, knickers. Keep calm for heaven's sake, take your time, stop fussing. Now go out slowly and lock the door, have I got the car keys? For Christ's sake don't fall down that step, fifty times I've meant to get that outside light fixed. The whole site was in darkness, there wasn't a soul about. I got in the car and headed up for Bernie's but a few yards down the main road my knees started knocking and nothing would stop them, I had to pull off the road and sit hanging on to the wheel while they beat each other uncontrollably. All I needed was for my teeth to join in in sympathy, but they were so tightly clenched together they couldn't move. At last the shaking stopped and I was able to make it the rest of the way up the road.

'I thought you'd be back tonight,' she said as she opened the door, 'I told you to stay, but of course you wouldn't.'

'I think I've started.'

'And not before your bloody time. Are the pains bad? Will you have a cup of tea?'

'No, but I'd love coffee — the pains aren't very bad at all. I think I'll go to bed here for a while, there's no point in going in too early.'

'All right, but make sure that you call us whenever you are ready. Brian will drive you.'

I slept fitfully, waking every time a big pain grabbed me. They were definitely getting worse. I'll get up after the next one, I kept promising myself, it's not good to be in hospital too soon, everyone says it's better to stay at home as long as possible. Definitely I'll get up after the next one.

'Do you realise it is ten o'clock in the morning, are you ever going to get out of that bed — do you want that child to be born here?' It was Bernie standing beside the bed with a cup of tea. 'Hurry up now, Brian is ready to drive you. You're still having the pains?' she asked anxiously, as I appeared to be making no effort to move.

'Yes I am,' I reassured her, 'in fact they have been fairly bad for quite some time.' She left and I struggled up and got dressed with an effort. The pains were bad, grabbing me like a vice and making me want to scream. Finally I got down the stairs. Brian was standing in the hall, trying hard not to look nervous.

'Right, I'm ready then, see you soon,' I called back to Bernie as we went out the door. I waved to her from the car as she stood there with her children. On the way down the road, I remembered that my television wasn't working, so I persuaded Brian to drop by the caravan to collect it and drop it in at the repair shop on our way to town. He looked at me as if I had gone completely mad, but seemed to think it was better to humour me, so we dragged the big heavy television set out of the caravan between us and got it into the car. I looked around for other things to do. I really should do the washing-up and clean up the kitchen . . . In the end, Brian caught me and practically forced me into the car. The pains were coming fairly fast, the traffic was fairly bad. I could see a line of perspiration on Brian's upper lip, and his hands clenched on the wheel, every time we got stuck at traffic lights. At last we turned into Hatch Street and found the nursing home without any bother.

I begged Brian not to leave me and he came in, though I could see that it was with great reluctance. Bernie had warned me that when he brought her in to have their babies, he dropped her at the door and ran. The nursing home was spread over two Georgian houses and it was a long time since anything had been done to it; its splendour was a thing of the past. We sat silent, maybe I shouldn't have come, I was probably too soon, they would send me home again . . .

'Will you come this way please, Mrs. O'Mahony,' a middle aged nurse led me away to a room on the second floor. 'Get undressed and get into bed and I will be back in a minute.'

The room was small and rectangular, with a very high ceiling, the elaborate cornices on two corners, but missing on the opposite two where it had been divided. The iron bed stood in the middle, facing two high windows, a wash basin in between them. A table, a chair and wardrobe, and beside the bed a tiny cot, all covered in pretty coloured cloth, a mixture of pinks, blues and yellows. They were taking no chances. The bed was so high that I could only get up on it by rolling myself on from my side. I lay there thinking how shabby and run down the whole place was. The nurse came back.

'Well you certainly picked the right day to come,' she said with an effort not to sound too unpleasant. 'Every room is full, we're run off our feet, now if you had come yesterday you would have had us all to yourself.'

I apologised for my lack of consideration, and winced

as she stuck her fingers into me.

'That baby is coming along fine, shouldn't take very long to arrive at all, the head is well down. I'm going to give you an enema now, wait about ten minutes and then empty your bowels over there.' She pointed to a covered commode which I hadn't noticed in the corner and then she was gone. I could hear no sound from any other room, I was deserted and alone, entombed in a square box. I tried hard to keep the panic and rejection at bay. They were very busy, the nurse said, it wasn't because I was single that I was being left alone, if I had come yesterday the nurse would have stayed with me, but she couldn't today. My insides contracted and I shot off the bed so fast I nearly landed on my belly. I just made it to the commode when everything inside me turned to liquid and ran out of me. I felt sure the baby and all must be gone. The pains were getting very bad, I was whimpering with pity for myself when the nurse returned and told me to get up on the bed, she wanted to shave me. I struggled up on the bed and was no sooner there than the urge to shit made me roll off again. If I shit all over the bed, that would be the end of it — to be an unmarried mother was one thing, to shit all over the bed was something else, they would put me out on the street.

Back on the bed again, I had to lie with my legs spread while I was shaved. Efficiently and unemotionally, with a bowl of water in one hand and a razor in the other she removed my precious hair — she didn't care, I bet she never had her hair removed, what if it didn't grow again? I'd be bald like a scalded crow. She was looking through the bag I had brought with me.

'Where is the gamgie wool and the rest of the things for the baby?' she asked.

'I don't know,' I stammered, what on earth was gamgie wool, and why hadn't I brought all the other things? Hadn't I got the list? Why hadn't I called for the list? I couldn't come in without the gamgie wool.

'Please,' I begged, 'I didn't know about the list and the gamgie wool. Maybe my friend downstairs could get them, if you gave him the list?'

The disapproval on her face would have stopped a grand-father clock, but she went away muttering, presumably to ask Brian to get the things for me. Before she went she told me that I was very tense, that there was no reason for me to be in such a state, that I should relax. To help me into that condition she gave me a jab of a needle into the backside. All it seemed to do was make me muzzy and weak. Just as I was in the middle of a huge contraction the door opened and Brian appeared with the gamgie wool, etc. and a look of pure fright on his face. As soon as he came near the bed I grabbed him and held on for dear life until the pain eased, but the minute I loosened my hold he was gone like a hare.

Nurse returned and examined me and tut-tutted because I wasn't dilating as much as I should be. Several times I screamed, clinging to her when the contractions got bad. She removed my hands from her, telling me there was no need for such hysterics. I got another shot in the back-side, and she went away and left me alone again.

Next time two nurses came, one on each side of me. I wasn't making any progress at all, I was very bad. They spoke across me as if I were totally deaf, but I could catch odd words. I tried to tell them that it didn't matter — I didn't mind dying, my baby would die too, but that was all right, couldn't be born with no gamgie wool, must have gamgie wool, should have sent for the list. I tried to tell them that I would prefer if they didn't talk about me as if I wasn't there, I didn't like that really.

'Push,' the nurse was saying, 'Put your feet against the palms of our hands and push.' When I pushed like that I could feel the thrust of the baby, but when they left me alone I had no strength, I tried, but the contractions were over by the time I had gathered my strength.

'So we got you at long last did we?' the door burst open and D'Arcy appeared like life itself, with the nurses in tow.

'So how are you doing? You're grand, you're grand, take it easy now child, you'll be fine, push hard, nurse go in there and help her to push. You are doing fine now, that baby will be here in no time. I have to go out now with my wife to afternoon tea, very grand people we are going to tea with, delicate bone china and pretty fingers of bread and butter, that you could starve to death while you'd be eating them. I'll have to sit there holding my cup with three fingers and crooking my little finger, to show that I was properly reared like all the best people. Then I'll tell them that I have an auld bitch above in the bed in labour and that I must go back to her and I'll leave them there with their little fingers sticking out and my wife threatening to divorce me for my vulgarity as soon as she gets me home.'

It isn't only his wife who will do something to him, I thought, as I watched the nurses flinch, but he carried on as though completely unaware that he might be offending them. 'There y'are now, you're a lovely sight, I'll be back before that baby comes, don't you worry, you are doing fine, it will be an excuse for me to get away from this other crowd of auld ones. I wouldn't go at all but my wife insists, thinks I've nothing better to be doing but drinking weak tea, out of weak cups. My God, women!' he muttered as he ambled out of the room. It was the only time I had ever heard him talk disdainfully about women. Even he had his limit it seemed.

He had been trying to cheer me up, I knew. For once he had failed completely, but I wasn't going to die. Nobody could die with him around.

After he had left the nurses stayed for a while and then had to go to some other patient. The contractions were strong but I couldn't push, poor baby, would never come out, tried my best but it wouldn't come out . . . nurses had left me . . . doctor had left me . . .

'Herald or Press, Mrs., Herald or Press?' An evening paper man had burst into the room and was waving a paper at me. I struggled up in the bed to get sixpence out of my bag. 'Press, Please,' I said. Through a haze of pain and drugs I could see his face — a middle-aged man, kind and jovial looking. Suddenly a huge contraction got me and I screamed. He realised that I was in the middle of labour and backed away saying,

'Oh Jaysus! Mrs., it's all right, Jaysus, don't worry yerself now about the money, yez can have the paper, sure the news is all bad anyway — sure nobody would want to read it — ah, God be good to ye . . . ' and he backed out the door.

I fell back exhausted. Why were the people who designed these places so stupid, I thought feebly. Surely if a woman who had a baby had had anything to do with it they would be different. If only there was a board at the end of the bed and a rope to hang on to I could bring my baby, I knew I could. But thrown on my back like this I had no leverage, maybe they made it that way deliberately so that women would die. If I could squat, if I could squat, I could do it. I tried to get up but the effort was too much. I couldn't bring my baby — they had all deserted me. Eric. My sister. The nurses. The doctor. Even the paper man had run away. Poor baby, nurse said you couldn't come without the gamgie wool. Why would you come anyway? Nobody wanted you, nobody except me. My nine hundred years was over and I was going to die, and nobody in the whole world cared . . .

'Oh that poor child, put her out quickly!' I heard the doctor's voice. A nurse came towards me and something came down over my face.

XXVIII

'Wake up Mrs. O'Mahony, you have a grand baby,' Someone was shaking me. I didn't want to talk about babies, I wanted to go to sleep. 'Go away and leave me alone,' I growled. 'I want to go to sleep.' But the gentle persistent shaking and a soft voice got to me.

'Mrs. O'Mahony, Mrs. O'Mahony, wake up, don't you want to see your daughter?'

A daughter! A *daughter*? That was me they were talking to! I opened my eyes. A young nurse was bending over me. She propped the pillows up behind my head and out of nowhere produced a bundle and plonked it on my shoulder. My child, my daughter. I peeped at her. She was a tiny little thing, all snugly wrapped and only her face showing. My God! It was as if you had cut the head off her father, she was the spitten image of him. Big blue eyes, wide open and alert, staring straight at me as though she knew much more about the whole scene than I ever would. I lay there with her on my shoulder, terrified to move in case she would break or disappear. Gingerly I moved around and managed to get her into my arms. She stared at me, yawned and closed her eyes, as if she had decided everything was in order and she could afford to go to sleep now. Without thinking I started singing her my favourite Paul Robeson lullaby.

'Oh, my baby, my curly headed baby,
I'll sing you fast asleep.'

The nurse laughed and came over, she moved back the blanket from the little head — my baby had a crop of straight black hair hanging down to her neck. The nurse lifted her from my arms and laid her in the cot.

'I am going to take her away now, you take these pills, they will make you sleep, and you need it, you have had a very hard time. Rest now.'

'But the baby! When will you bring her back?'

'Don't you worry, I'll take her down to the nursery now, she'll be back in the morning, we'll take good care of her. You go to sleep now.'

YIPPEEEEE — ! I have a daughter, a beautiful darling daughter! I have survived, I'm not dead at all, and my baby isn't dead. I sat up in bed. What time was it? There wasn't a sound anywhere. It couldn't be very late. God, what had happened to my daughter? Why had they taken her away? Maybe I'd never get her back . . . God, hurry up and let it be morning! Sleep, the nurse had said, how could I sleep? I sang a bit of a song. My voice sounded strange in the drab silence. But I was sitting on a cloud above the bed. I had a daughter — the rush of love for that tiny little person completely astonished me. I had promised myself I would love the child, expecting to do it in a dutiful unemotional way, but I was completely overwhelmed — every urge to love that I had ever had rushed out and was centered on that tiny mite. Why couldn't they bring her back to me? I slept and woke and sang and giggled, hugged myself in the excitement of the enormous love that was flooding me.

At last a tiny hint of light between the curtains. I got out of bed and washed myself as best I could, got dressed and waited. Surely it wouldn't be long now? The nurse nearly had a fit when she came in and found me all dressed and ready to go.

'Good God, Mrs. O'Mahony, get back into that bed this minute, don't you realise you have only just had a baby and you have had a pretty bad time, it is only six o'clock, where on earth do you think you are going? Come on now,' she said more gently, leading me to the bed and helping me to get undressed again.

'Do you think they will bring my baby soon?' I asked, trying not to let her know that by now I was convinced someone had stolen the child.

'We must clean you up now first,' she said, disappearing and returning with a bed bath which she shoved under me with practised ease.

'Take it easy now, you have got a lot of stitches, this water is salted and we will have to wash you with it until you can have a bath, nothing like the bit of salt and water to cure what ails you.'

She poured water over me from a jug, just above my hair line and letting it run down between my legs, warm, soothing, gentle, healing. She removed the bath and dried me like a baby, and then at last I discovered what the gamgie wool was about, it was a huge roll of thick cotton wool, much more absorbent than STs it seemed. She put a big wad of it in between my legs, slipped a pair of knickers over it and covered me up. I was sitting up on my cloud again watching these proceedings with interest.

'You can order your breakfast now in a minute,' she said and was gone before I could ask, 'but what about the baby?'

At last a nurse brought her in. She was fed, bathed and changed. The cot was put beside the bed and I was able to examine her. She was perfect, brown skin, not a bit wrinkled or scrawny. She was asleep, but as if she knew I needed it she opened her eyes and stared at me without blinking. She knew all about me, I could see, I didn't have to explain myself to her, she was as old as the world. The minute the nurse's back was turned, I got her out of the cot and up on the pillow. I snuggled down against her, I was safe, she was with me. I slept the sleep of total exhaustion.

XXIX

They all came in the afternoon, Susan and Joan, Betty, Tom and Sheila, Áine, Bernie and Brian. The little room was full, they brought flowers and cards, clothes for the baby, drinks and fruit. The communal feeling of achievement could be felt, we had succeeded, this wasn't just my baby, we all had a stake in her. Susan suggested that we had better get a name for her, but I was totally confused. No matter what they came up with I turned it down, no name was good enough for my child. Betty had the baby in her arms gurgling and cooing to her when the nurse swept in and removed her, giving us a lecture on how bad it was to take the child up like that. We listened, suitably subdued, but as soon as she was gone, Áine lifted the baby back into bed to me. They all left, relieved that it was all over and they could relax.

The doctor came, obviously pleased to see me in such good form. Earlier one of the nurses had told me that only for him I could have been in labour for another twelve hours. She said it, I felt, as though she thought that would have been much more suitable to my status than all this attention I seemed to be getting.

'Some hard time you gave us,' D'Arcy was saying, 'You got very sick when we gave you that chloroform, you know, several nurses had to hold on to you. Are those stitches sore yet?'

'Not in the least bit,' I answered carelessly, 'I can't

even feel them.'

'You will, my girl, you will, you are well stitched, trussed up like a chicken ready for the oven, oh you'll feel them all right. Do you know that is one of the most alert babies I have delivered in forty years, looked straight up at me she did, the minute I took her out, intelligent child. But you are a nice one, when you were under the chloroform you told all the nurses I was the father, there's a thing to do to me, a respectable man in my position.' He was gabbling away, pleased with his own wit, but in a flash it came to me.

'Oh well, if I told the nurses all that, I had better prove it, I'm going to call her Darina after you – and I'll tell them that too.'

I wished that I could tell him how grateful I was, how I had felt that I was dying and he had dragged me back. But the words would have been hopeless and I kept up the banter. I could say nothing but take it all, and somehow, somewhere I'd give it all back. Taking in, giving out, passing the strength around one to another.

'Oh well, I suppose everyone will say I am the father now,' he said, trying to sound disgruntled, but evidently tickled and not caring a damn what anyone thought. And why shouldn't he be the father? He had done more to give my child life than the man who had carelessly spilled his seed into me.

By the second day the routine of the nursing home became clear. 7 am, wake and wash; 8 am, breakfast; 10 am, baby brought; 10.30, snack; 12 noon, lunch; 3 pm, snack; 5 pm, dinner; 7 pm, baby taken away; 8 pm, wash; 10 pm, cocoa, pills and lights out. I enjoyed every minute of it. By the second day I had also found out about the stitches. Lying on the bed was a nightmare, but trying to sit on a chair was even worse: the bathing every day was the only relief. The two older nurses, O'Brien and Hickey, came on during the day. They seemed to blend with the surroundings of the nursing home, not really very old, but somehow worn out and frayed. In the night there was the young nurse with the gentle voice whose name I never learned. O'Brien and Hickey upbraided me daily because I had brought no nappies with me. Susan got me a dozen, but she should have got the bigger size, they said, and anyway she should have got two dozen. On about the third day I was told I could have a bath. O'Brien helped me upstairs to the bathroom and washed me as if I was completely helpless.

The joy of having Darina was growing so that I thought I'd burst asunder. As soon as the nurse had left her in the morning I whipped her into bed with me, except for when she was taken off for feeding and changing. I felt no regret that I wasn't feeding her. When I decided that I must keep my job, I also realised that that cut out breast feeding; neither did I have any objection to their feeding or changing her. All I wanted to do was hold her and talk to her and sing, all of which she seemed to like. The nurses gave up taking her out of the bed and putting her back in her cot. Sometimes they knocked on the door because they thought I had visitors when they heard me talking or singing to the child. Suddenly, at around six o'clock, she would let out the most ungodly yell, and nothing would stop her for half an hour or more. That such a tiny thing could yell so loud astonished me. All I could do was hold her and talk quietly to her, which sometimes seemed to calm her for a little while, but then she would gaze at me suspiciously and start all over again. Apart from that, she was perfect. She listened intently while I sang to her, and obviously appreciated all the stories I told her about the caravan, about our friends, about Edith. I had become very expert at handling her wrapped up in her blanket, but one day it came off and there she was, a tiny bitty thing that was all spindly arms and legs. My heart did a somersault: what on earth would I do with her? She started screaming, wrinkling up her face and getting redder and redder, letting me know that she disapproved of my incompetence. There was nothing I could do. I explained to her as best I could that I just didn't know how to get the blanket back around her again the way the nurses did. The more I tried, the more her little clothes became ruffled, until they were all up around her neck and shoulders and I thought she would get strangled.

Nurse Hickey appeared, snatched the child, wrapped her up again just by flicking her fingers, and bore her away.

My breasts swelled until I couldn't bear the pain. I dragged myself up the stairs and toppled into the bath. Kneeling there and leaning forward on my hands with the enormous objects submerged in the warm salty water brought some relief. If I rocked very gently, the water lapped around the stitches and the pendulous, swollen breasts were soothed as well. I would never have believed that my tiny breasts could reach such Junoesque proportions, or that the process could be so painful. The skin was tight and stretched and sore, the nipples standing up hard. The sides of my breasts actually got in the way of my arms; every now and again I touched them accidentally and nearly screamed. Ever since my early teens I had always longed for big boobs . . .

I had been five days in the nursing home and no one else had come to see me, but I didn't really mind. I loved the security of it, having my meals served in bed, the long chats with the baby, the naps with her snuggled up on my shoulder, having her taken away so that I could get a good night's sleep and brought back all fresh and fed in the morning. The attitudes of Hickey and O'Brien seemed to have changed towards me. At first I thought, they had decided that an unmarried mother who could afford to have her child in a private nursing home must be a brazen bitch who was being kept by a man. Now they were kindness itself.

Several days earlier I had been given forms to fill in for the registration of the baby. I had hedged from day to day, refusing to do it. I couldn't face the fact that any place where 'Father' was marked, I would have to leave blank. As far as officialdom was concerned, my child had no father.

'Can I have those forms please,' Hickey said, automatically reaching to take Darina out of the bed and then deciding it was a waste of time. 'It's all right, child,' she carried on, seeing my hesitation, 'I know you are not married — don't worry, no one will see it.' Her face was alive with kindness and understanding and I wondered how I had ever thought her a frustrated auld bitch. 'You needn't be afraid to talk to O'Brien and myself. You have a place of your own to take the child, I heard.'

'Yes,' I said eagerly, telling her about the caravan and how Bernie would mind her and how I'd be able to keep my job. It all bubbled out in the relief of being able to drop the pretence of a husband hanging around somewhere. 'Does everybody know I'm not married?' I couldn't resist asking.

'No, only O'Brien and myself. The doctor told us when he hired us to nurse you. He is a great man, we've nursed with him for twenty years, nobody knows what that man has done for people . . . ' She trailed off. Twenty years of D'Arcy couldn't have been dull. I was bursting to ask her questions, but that would have been an intrusion, so we stayed silent, united in admiration of our idol. At last she came back to earth.

'Oh well, I'd better get on,' she said, moving to the door. 'Don't you worry about this form, you have a beautiful child, and you'll have luck with her, indeed you will.'

Susan came with money. She had cashed my salary cheque for me, so I had enough to pay the nursing home. She also brought a letter from the boss, which was supposed to have been posted to my brother's home, where I was now officially staying recovering from my shingles. In the euphoria of Darina's birth I had written telling him that my shingles were now nearly gone, that I had had my first bath for weeks, and that I hoped to be back in the office in at least a fortnight. His reply was equally effusive, assuring me that he was delighted to hear from me, that it was great that I was better and warning me not to dream of coming back to work until I was completely cured. Susan and I shared the achievement of carrying all this subterfuge off successfully, and she filled me in on the office gossip, which as usual was totally uninteresting. I told her that I would be going home on Saturday, that Bernie had insisted that I must go to their house for a few days, so that she could look after me, and that they would come and collect me.

O'Brien and Hickey turned me over on my side and snipped the stitches. I felt so great that I asked them to show me how to wash and change the baby. O'Brien brought in the bath and towel and flannel and told me to fire ahead. I placed Darina on the bed and managed to take off her little cardigan without breaking her twiggy arms. While I wrestled with the knots on her long white gown she started getting restless. Eventually that came off, too, and we were down to the vest and nappy. That's where the trouble started. Instead of taking her arms out first, I tried to pull the vest over her head, nearly strangling her in the process. She roared her disapproval. Next I must get her into the bath without letting go of her. I tested the water with my elbow; it seemed to be all right. Gingerly I lifted the tiny body and lowered her into the water, my arm properly around her shoulders, holding her left arm firmly. In a flash she had twisted around like a miniature Houdini, her legs where her head had been, her head nearly under the water and me twisting her arm off. She screamed blue murder. I lost all sense of what was going on and was completely incapable of even lifting the child out of the water. O'Brien took over, washed her down and soothed her. She placed her on a towel on the bed and told me to dry and powder her, warning me to dry the folds of her flesh, under her arms and behind her knees and between her legs.

It was the first time I had looked at the baby properly; she was six days old and I had never seen her body. She was long and skinny, but somehow together. Her legs seemed to be twice the length of her body – perfect, every little detail perfect, all the toes and fingers and ears and nose, and the long black hair spread out wet on the towel.

'How is it that her colour has changed so much?' I asked

O'Brien, 'She was beautifully brown when she was born.'

'Oh God! all mothers are the same,' she sighed and shook her head in despair. 'Ye all think yeer babies had sunray lamps in there. The child was slightly jaundiced, that's all, most babies are born like that.' I was suitably deflated.

'Powder her up now and get her dressed. Come on, it's no use me doing it, you are going to have to manage yourself anyway when you go home. Hurry up now or she'll get pneumonia.'

Putting on her nappy was simple — there was nothing to it but to fold the nappy in a triangle, raise the child by the legs and slip it under her bum. No problem, I made the triangle all right, but in lifting her legs I jerked her so hard that I had her standing on her head. The nappy doubled up and I couldn't straighten it out. Darina screeched, O'Brien clicked her tongue sadly.

'Try again,' she said. I tried again.

After many false starts, I succeeded at last in getting some semblance of a well tied nappy, slipped the plastic pants on, held my darling daughter up in the air in triumph — and the whole lot, pants and nappy fell down on the floor. After O'Brien had left, I cried at the sheer hopelessness of trying to be a mother.

The next day I was running a fierce temperature and they wouldn't let me home.

On Sunday I was normal again and I was told I could go as soon as D'Arcy had seen me. I was dressed and ready by ten in the morning, but he didn't come until after lunch. He said I could go, and I rang Bernie and told her to come for me.

D'Arcy assured me that I would eventually learn to to bath the baby and change nappies. Contrary to popular belief, he didn't think it came naturally. There was an absurd pressure on mothers to know instinctively how to deal with every aspect of their baby's life. Instinct might play a large part in the emotional or spiritual life, but there was nothing natural about babies wearing nappies, so why should anyone have an instinct about how to put the bloody things on? That made me feel much more cheerful.

Hickey insisted on bringing Darina down to the door for me, and stood waving with O'Brien and D'Arcy as we drove away.

XXX

Betty and her children were in Bernie's to welcome us. Everyone pressed around Darina and fussed over her. She took it all in her stride and slept soundly. Betty had brought me the carry cot in which, as she said, she had reared three of hers. I was bitterly disappointed that she hadn't tried to clean it up or make it pretty. It was battered and beaten, the hood was all broken and it was grimy from having been stored in her attic. If my child had a father she wouldn't have to sleep in that old wreck . . .

When it came to feeding time, all the experts were intent on having their say, and I was equally intent on feeding my child myself. I was completely uptight and determined that no one was going to help me. I could get one side of the teat over the rim of the bottle, but each time I tried to pull it down all around, it would fly off and fall on the floor. Then it had to be washed and sterilised all over again, much to everyone's amusement. Darina was screaming to be fed, I was on the verge of tears, Betty was calling me a fuckin' eejit for not letting someone else do it, and in the end her mother took the child and the bottle and did it herself. I was feeling utterly tired and deflated. I really wanted to be at home, alone with my baby, but I couldn't manage to say that to Bernie. I went to bed as soon as I could. It was my first time sharing my room with Darina in her cot.

The weather was incredible. To greet my child there

was an Indian Summer. It was beautiful as only October can be when the sun shines and the leaves are turning. We drove the next day to my brother's house. It was a journey of about fifty miles, and every time the car stopped Darina opened her eyes and yowled. As soon as it started again, she slept.

Eddie's children all fussed about the baby and took photographs and carried her all over the place and *terrified* me. I was sure they would let her fall. If they had any questions about her father they kept them to themselves. I realised it must have been difficult for Eddie and Grace to deal with the situation, especially with the older children, but they had managed very well and there was no sign of embarrassment or uneasiness. We spent a pleasant afternoon there, and they reminded me that I was invited to come and stay whenever I wished.

On our way home, within a couple of miles of Dublin, Darina, who had been asleep in her cot, suddenly let out the most blood-curdling yell. I started shaking uncontrollably.

'Pull off the road quickly,' Bernie said, 'She has had some class of a fit, or something is sticking in her.' She got into the back seat and examined the child by the interior light of the car. There wasn't a mark on her, she was sleeping soundly. 'She must have been dreaming,' said Bernie as she climbed back into her own seat. Strange, I thought, to start having nightmares at a few days old.

I wanted to go home. I couldn't really rest in Bernie's place, I was under an obligation to be up helping in the house and with her children, and I just didn't feel well. My back was breaking and I was bleeding like a stuck pig, I was tired all the time and I had started crying. Every-time someone looked crooked at me, I cried. It wasn't a sobbing or convulsive crying, it wasn't because of anything I felt, in fact it seemed to have nothing to do with me at all. The water just poured down my face and nothing would stop it. Every time I said to Bernie that I wanted to go home she somehow persuaded me to stay another day, but by Thursday I had had enough. I was going home.

In the afternoon I took Bernie's two children, and, leaving Darina with her, I went down to the caravan to light the fire and heat up the place before I brought the baby down. I was feeling better already. At home I could stay in bed as long as I liked and relax and get my strength back. Darina and I could be together, I had so many songs to sing her and so many tales to tell her. We would change around the furniture and make room for her cot in the bedroom and sort out all the presents she had got, and buy whatever other odds and ends we needed. I wouldn't go back to work for another week, I decided, they had waited so long for me now, another week wouldn't kill them. The sun was pouring down on us, the caravan site looked almost pretty in the late October light . . .

'Is your name Brig O'Mahony?' a voice said from behind me, as I was going up the steps to the door. My heart stopped. Who knew my name? I had kept it a secret. But it was only the woman from the caravan above mine.

'I just wanted to let you know,' she said. 'They are clearing the site. They came while you were away. They left your notice in to me. All the vans has to be off the site by Monday, or they'll charge us a hundred pound a day and summons us to court and we'll be forcibly removed. A few of them has got sites elsewhere, but they're very hard to get and it costs a fortune to get the caravan towed. I just don't know what we're going to do. Have you another place to go?'

I looked at her without seeing her. Did she have any conception of what she was saying? Of course she was upset herself — everyone on the site must be — but now she was destroying all my dreams. My only hope of a home was that caravan. How could I be expected to start all over again in my condition, and find another shelter for me and the child? No, I couldn't do it. The tears started again. Oh, Christ, this really was the fucking end.

If you have enjoyed reading this book, you may be interested in some recent Ward River Press bestsellers, listed in the following pages.

First Time in Paperback

Eilís Dillon

THE BITTER GLASS

Another powerful novel, set in the West of Ireland, during the Civil War, by one of the country's most distinguished writers. A group of young people, cut off in Connemara by IRA action, are forced to come to terms with life and death. As the plot builds to its inevitable climax, their haunting experiences change their lives and their hopes forever. This is a disturbing and unforgettable book.

'*The Bitter Glass* . . . has a rounded excellence which comes from a mature technique and imagination of high quality. Without being in the least overwritten or sentimental, this is a most poetical book.'
The Times

'An excellent piece of work . . . full of reality, full of poetry, written with a very sure and sensitive hand. I was completely won by it . . . the world of Connemara was flawlessly conveyed . . . I was never more at home in a book.'
Eudora Welty

IR£2.75*
UK£2.50
0 907085 07 5
*Includes VAT

Another Ward River Bestseller!

Val Dorgan
CHRISTY RING

A Personal Portrait

Fast-moving, frank, full of excitement and fresh revelations, this is a deeply personal portrait of Cork's greatest hurler. Val Dorgan, seasoned journalist and former Glen Rovers team-mate of Christy Ring, brings his own unique brand of insight and reminiscence to make a truly memorable tribute.

'The controversy about whether the book should be published at all or not, assures the publishers of a "best seller" on their hands, and once bought, the book makes compulsive reading. . . I found I could not leave it down. . . This book to me enhances Christy's reputation (if that is possible). . . the man emerges from the book with an abundance of fine qualities.'

EDDIE KEHER, Sunday Independent

A Paperback Original, illustrated

IR£3.30*
UK£3.00
ISBN 0 907085 06 7
* includes VAT

Another Ward River Bestseller!

Christina Murphy

SCHOOL REPORT

The Guide To Irish Education for Parents, Teachers and Students

Over the past ten years, Irish education has changed almost beyond recognition. Here at last, Christina Murphy of *The Irish Times* answers all the vital questions, explains the current situation and future trends, and provides sound advice on a host of topics including:

Which school? National or Private? Secondary, Vocational, Community? Who owns our schools? How can parents take part in school management? How does the 'points' system work? What is the New Curriculum? What about religion and sex education? Which careers are open to school leavers? And many other topics.

With 256 pages and 27 tables giving all the facts and figures, this is the most useful guide to the system ever published. If you have a child at school, then you need SCHOOL REPORT.

A Paperback Original
ISBN 0 907085 00 8
UK £2.00
IR £2.20 including VAT

'An invaluable resource book' Forum, RTE

Another Ward River Bestseller!

Pan Collins
IT STARTED ON THE LATE LATE SHOW

A Paperback Original

What lies behind the smooth professionalism of Gay Byrne's Late Late Show? Has it really changed Irish society? How is this fantastically successful TV show actually put together?

Pan Collins, senior researcher, tells the backroom story of the men and women behind the Late Late Show. How it began. The early years. What Gay Byrne is like to work with. The team. The recipe for success. What happens when an international star fails to turn up on the night.

The big names are all here: James Mason, Michael Mac Liammoir, Oliver Reed, Mary Whitehouse. So too are all the details of "specials" like the Toy Show, the "penguin" show and the 500th Late Late Show. But Ireland sees itself mirrored in the Late Late Show, and the most explosive audience reaction has come when the Show tackled such delicate issues as parapsychology, lesbianism and the taxation of farmers.

For wit, warmth and sheer readibility, Pan Collins has written the showbiz book of the decade.

ISBN 0 907085 00 8
IR£2.75*
UK£2.50

*includes VAT